CDN

December 2019

**Book One**

**of**

**The Flying Crooked Series**

**GEOFF NELDER**

SUPPOSE WE

# SUPPOSE WE

Paperback version

© 2019 by Geoff Nelder
ISBN: 978-0-9975549-3-9

Published in the USA by LL-Publications 2019
www.ll-publications.com
PO Box 542
Bedford
Texas 76095

Edited by Billye Johnson
Book layout and typesetting by jimandzetta.com
Cover design by jimandzetta.com

*Suppose We* is a work of fiction. The names, characters, and incidents are entirely the work of the author's imagination. Any resemblance to actual persons, living or dead, or events, is entirely coincidental.

# GEOFF NELDER'S
# BOOKS

Humorous thriller *ESCAPING REALITY.*

Award-winning science fiction mystery with a hot-blooded heroine, *EXIT, PURSUED BY A BEE.*

Another thriller, *HOT AIR*, received an Award d'Or from an Arts Academy in the Netherlands.

A science fiction trilogy, *ARIA* with an original premise is published by LL-Publications. It won the P&E readers poll in 2012.

An experimental science fiction story released as an ebook, *THE CHAOS OF MOKII.*

Historical fantasy, *XAGHRA'S REVENGE* is set in the Maltese islands and based on a true mass abduction of the people of Gozo in 1551.

*INCREMENTAL* is a collection of 25 of Geoff Nelder's more surreal short stories.

# Dedication

Gaynor, Geoff's wife, will not read his stories she says, in case she finds herself as a character. She isn't and yet in some ways she is, for without her support and bemused tolerance this novel would not have been written. Dedicated also to son, Rob, daughter, Eleanor, and to their marvellous families.

# Travellers' Notes

All the characters in this tale are fictional. The organic and inorganic lifeforms in the Keplerian system on the other hand are as real as I am sitting here, on a fence.

For those readers who enjoy exploring fiction via the real world they will find the Kepler 20 system really exists although the Kepler-20h planet has yet to be spotted. If you point your fingers between Cygnus and Lyra, they'll be in the right direction for the location of this story. As a geographer, I relish locational accuracy but here I allowed my imagination to soar with a strange new world.

As a child, I loved reading those space exploration stories. Already this planet was becoming too limited for my developing imagination. Luckily, there were hundreds of science fiction authors with strange planets in their heads for me to explore. My tastes have become subtler but I still enjoy reading and watching movies that explore new vistas in outer space. Hence this book realises a lifelong urge to paint my own vision of what a strange yet habitable planet might be like. I enjoy breaking tropes. For example the natives, instead of attacking the human 'invaders' are so far ahead they ignore them. Think how far we've advanced in the last century, now imagine how far we'll be in a million years! Rare in the books I've read are ecosystems where there are no predators larger than insects, until I wrote this one.

# SUPPOSE WE

**Flying Crooked**
The butterfly, the cabbage white,
(His honest idiocy of flight)
Will never now, it is too late,
Master the art of flying straight,
Yet has – who knows so well as I? –
A just sense of how not to fly:
He lurches here and here by guess
And God and hope and hopelessness.
Even the aerobatic swift
Has not his flying crooked gift.

Robert Graves

# FOREWORD

A lilac butterfly alighted on my laptop. I was in my favourite writing spot: outdoors with the sound of the Mediterranean Ocean lapping a stony beach, me and the computer barely keeping sufficiently cool to function. Yet, there it was. A delicate creature flapping its wings at page 39 demanding to be let in. So I did. The thing is, it grew on me and became a kind of silent character. An alien butterfly yet it wasn't really a butterfly as you will see.

This novella takes you to outer space, to a planetary system in the Milky Way that the Kepler orbiting satellite discovered. I've always devoured stories of astronauts discovering strange planets, things going wrong and how would *I* cope? Kepler-20h is very strange. Surprises around each twisted tower and creatures so intelligent they ignore the humans even when they're desperate. However, we've not arrived there yet... nearly....

# CHAPTER ONE

A blue spot of sunlight found its way through a viewport, flickered around the cockpit and woke up Gaston Poirer. He'd only been asleep for three hours, unlike his three-member crew, immersed in their dreamtime for months. They weren't supposed to dream in suspension, but he did, or perhaps only in the last second or so. After all, his thoughts travelled at one twenty metres per second and his fantasies faster, in their crooked flight.

No wonder he fell asleep. This module was a cross between an actor's green room and a padded cell. A psycho-designers' experiment. He tapped for the sleep log and grunted. He must have missed Em's doodles: yellow petals on the console's margins during her shift. How unprofessional, just wait until Commander Penn sees it. He'd go ballistic, but then they all were, literally.

Umm, he'd assumed it was time for shift change, but he must have napped. What alerted him? Presumably not the spilt coffee aroma on his SpaceWeb T-shirt, a blue world image now sporting the invasion of a mud monster. Ah, *oui* the uncertain light in his eyes. So soon? It should have taken 1062 years for the *Suppose We* to reach the Kepler-20 system.

He checked the navigation status. Yes, that's Kepler-20, humanity's hoped-for future system, but the planet Kepler-20h, their target remained months away.

The AI—still largely dumb after a malfunction—must have wanted him not to remain dozing at his post and turned the cockpit eight degrees to allow that distant sun, a mere pinprick, to peep at him. Why not the other alert systems? He ran a diagnostics check. He'd been pinged and vibrated. Some deep nap. Maybe intermittent hibernation over a thousand years had residual snoozing as one of its side effects, or it was just him. Age had crept up on him, after all theoretically he could celebrate his one thousandth and eighty-seventh birthday tomorrow.

He waved fingers at the console to pick up those alerts. Proximity threat. His stomach tightened but there was nothing nearby on radar. He checked X-ray and infrared along with the rest of the electromagnetic spectrum. *Que fais-tu?* False alarms had dogged this flight although some had been dealt with by *Suppose We* without human interaction: one comet avoidance and a green iridescent gas cloud for which the AI decided to hold our breath and plough through rather than a lengthy detour.

Unlike in the movies there was no engine hum. The quasi-Alcubierre drive was shaped as a ring and warped spacetime just in front of *Suppose We* pulling the needle-shaped ship through the universe at point eight lightspeed. The only wings were forcefield deltas deployed in orbit. They wouldn't rattle. Gaston heard the odd gurgle from recycling and life support, but it was all green.

He should investigate further. Double check the sensors, run through cam footage and—hello, *qu'est-ce que c'est?* The cockpit swung again, like a tank turret, changing the viewport view from the blue sun to a blank piece of sky. Should it be blank? He pulled up a star map, nothing much to see in that direction. A red light came on dead-centre and threw itself into a blinking frenzy.

Was this a pivotal moment when he should wake up Penn such as an alien contact? No, it was probably a glitch, and what would the bearded wonder do? Send out rapid Quantum Mech probes fore and aft to triangulate time decoherences. He could do that. No one understood how they worked anyway.

Off they went. He couldn't see them, the size of marbles and no doubt tinier ones were on their way from Earth using cusps, leap-frogging space to get to Kepler before them. Marbles loaded with people, somehow. What a waste of time this trip was. Ah, a ping turned into a frantic dinging. The QM beasties have found a mass where everything said there was nothing and it was coming at them. He should be more excited than when Fransesca Dupont sat on his lap at a concert, but sadly, Earth's experience of its first contact ended badly, if it ended at all.

In the Oort cloud, a remotely-controlled SpaceWeb explorer craft detected an alien ship, shaped like a croissant and the size of the Arc de Triumph. Its hatch was open, no one aboard. Earth Control signalled the explorer craft to tow the alien ship back to

Moon orbit. The media repeatedly screamed warnings about Trojan Horses, however, it exploded near Neptune, along with the Earth craft. Analysis of sensor data continued for centuries with no agreed conclusions. Gaston was in the accident camp, Penn in the evil-alien camp, which possessed far more followers. He would. Penn's younger brother was in the destroyed explorer ship.

Gaston examined the data from the QM marbles. Insufficient data with a range of possibilities. Sadly for Penn, and maybe for Gaston, it was wakey-wakey time.

☉ ✗ ☉

There was no rapid waking from hibernation. It took a day to drain, refill, remove the wax, massage, stimulate those dormant parts that preferred to stay out of it. Luckily, for everyone, Gaston wasn't personally involved. By the time Penn had assumed his usual belligerent intelligence, *Suppose We* had made three course alterations, but the invisible object changed too and closed in.

The commander reminded Gaston of lollipop trees: a mass of auburn hair and beard on stick torso and legs, reeking of ammonia from the cleanser. His American – apparently Seattle – accent became stronger with rage. "Why the hell didn't you wake me earlier?"

A French bottom lip stuck out in reply.

Penn poked at console screens. Freckled white fingers tipped with overgrown nails making Gaston shiver. "So it's a blasted stealth ship? And let's have proper answers."

"Is it?"

"Well, man, we can't see the damned thing."

Gaston pointed at his own console. His own natural-olive skin fingers with carefully trimmed nails. "Those marbles can, using infinitesimal time and space decoherences, so they are not that superior at remaining hidden."

Penn harrumphed and sat while sucking a wakeup tube, reminding Gaston to punch a request for double croissants with confiture and coffee.

The Commander grunted at Gaston, "Why can't our tiny spies see inside the mass? I'd like to see if it's a ship, a fleet or just a steered rock."

"The coffee smells *manifique*, but always comes out too soon."

A croissant found itself disappearing into Penn's starving maw, but spluttered out again. Just as well they have gravity – the bits floated downwards at three-quarters g. "Why isn't it gaining on us? And I see we've slowed to point six." He glared at Gaston, who decided against a Gallic shrug.

"I think they might be steering us, Sir."

"Really? By horse manure you're right, by making our AI manoeuvre an optimum escape route. Clever."

Gaston reached for the wake-up panel. "I should wake the women, *Oui*?"

"Not yet, two heads are better than four, and that Em with her constant nattering about home, scrambles my brain. How did she get a place on this mission?"

"Top of the class in nav and comms and you picked her. Not just because she is a blonde, no?"

Penn looked away while coughing into his hand. "Plan A. Turn off the auto AI nav, increase speed to our max point eight to the Kepler-20 sun following a projected intercept with planet h."

Gaston switched panels. "Coming at it out of the sun, to fool their detection strategies?"

"Sure, in one, why what d'you know?"

"That has been the AI choice all along and it redirects to it after the diverging from the mass following us."

Penn reached for coffee, downed it in one. "Okay, chief exo-linguist, exo-biologist, and exo-wiseguy, you've had more time than me. What's your plan?"

"A *petite* change, No, a big one. Leave now at right angles to our current trajectory for two or three weeks."

"Got you. Check if they're following, maybe sneak behind this stealth mass to find out more about it. Let me dwell on it... No."

Gaston slowly shook his head. He'd anticipated the commander's response. "Consider it, *mon ami*, Sir. What is a few weeks compared to the millennium we have travelled?"

"No and *Non*, Gaston. It's not that simple. Follow my screen." Penn used two fingers drawing red and blue lines that had animated numbers following trajectories. Gaston smirked with the memory of himself using his ambidextrous skills to conduct an orchestra with two batons. The Blue Danube had never sounded so chaotic on the right yet languid on the left.

"...furthermore... you're not damned listening, are you?"

"*Pardon*, but my eyes were listening. I see a week away would take four weeks to catch up because of their orbit and us not being able then to use Kepler-20 for slingshot manoeuvre. Our resources, though, are surplus. Checking yesterday, the hydroponics and protein trays are one hundred percent operative."

"Um, maybe so, but if that beast behind us follows and swallows us, we'll be even farther away from possible help from Kepler."

Gaston did a better job this time of keeping a straight face. "Help?"

Penn kept his face at his screen as he pulled up data from planet Kepler-20h. "Yeah, it was you, remember, who interpreted these radio spikes as signs of culture."

"Possibly, but they could just as well be random radio noise generated by natural events such as lightning. Let us divert for one hour. Then see what happens." Bartering had always been Gaston's strong point. He only needed one hour.

"Fine. Set it for twenty minutes time while I update the log."

Gaston glanced sideways at Penn, assessing his demeanour. Perhaps his increasing irascibility and overtly military hard line was a side effect of the hibernation.

☉ ✕ ☉

"Well, I'll be darned, they're *not* following us!"

"I did not think they would. We are nothing. They happened to be using our trajectory. *Oui*, maybe tweaking a little for reasons of their own, making our AI do little avoidance strategies."

Penn scratched his mop of red hair, sending fragments of hibernation wax and hair into the air. "They must be en route – hey see what I said there, my Parisian pal – to Kepler." His relief at *Suppose We* not being the obvious target manifested itself with a grin.

Waving Penn's musty slow-falling detritus towards a suction filter, Gaston refrained from suggesting a post-hiber-shower was overdue. "Perhaps they are neither friend nor foe. We need to stop thinking like humans."

"Whoa, since when has the damned cockpit started rotating like that?"

"Ah, I believe it is my fault." Gaston didn't want to admit to napping so deeply that the AI had to resort to physical manipulation for its alerts. "*Regardez*, the viewport. The red alert cross-hairs point to behind the stealth mass. *Merde*."

"Another one? Hang on, that's our marbles sending data back, but the AI must have known about the first one. How?"

"I really do not know. I've not had time to interrogate it. Outside the usual detection parameters. The marbles are able to see it with QM time decoherence differences, so perhaps it did too."

"Goddammit, Gaston, that first one is bigger than Jupiter! If that's an enemy then Kepler's in trouble and we've had a wasted journey."

Gaston waved his hands apart. "Might just be an echo. It is eighty light minutes away, approximately the same distance as our sun to Saturn. We have no idea if it has mass. Perhaps a light gas, or just a web entity."

"Or a cunningly disguised heavy-metal Death Star. We need to stop it."

Gaston wanted to sigh. "You know that if it was a Jupiter-size ferrous body, our petite craft will already have—"

"Yeah, experience perturbations from its gravity and it would be hard to disguise..."

"And stop, without detection, but we mustn't assume anything. Probably not a spaceship at that size. It could be a directed planet or... whatever, it is what it is."

"Yeah, right, but since we don't know what it is, my job is to assume they aren't friendly. They're obviously a threat to the Kepler system and so to Earth's hope for when we have to leave the home-world."

Gaston took a long breath. "How do you know they are a threat?"

Penn pointed, ironically, at the viewport. "Just look at them!"

A long exhale at the nothing-to-see gesture. "New data. There's another stealth following the first two. All eighty light-minutes apart, about a billion and a half k."

"Same size? Ah, we can't tell until the marbles travel back again. Now, look here, it could all be a dastardly coincidence that this wagon train of massive things are arriving at the same time as us, but we need to create a breathing space. Partly to establish ourselves on Kepler-20h and maybe warn any Keps that might be there."

"I hope you are not thinking—"

Penn stroked his hair back. "You think I'm thinking? Great, and maybe you'll think to agree that we have to do it."

"All right."

Penn's eyebrows danced a jig of surprise. "What, you agree?"

"*Oui,* I'll send the data for the current location and trajectories of the masses to Kepler-20h on all the bandwidths we can broadcast."

"Not that."

"*Non!* I cannot agree to an attempt to destroy the mass. At least let us try and communicate with it."

Penn's green eyes bored into the Frenchman. "We *cannot* alert them to our knowing about them."

"But they—"

"Already do, but not our military capability. Okay we couldn't destroy an iron Jupiter, but whatever we do will likely put them off their course, and make the rest hesitate too. We send off an imploder, its likely too small for them to see it coming. It won't generate a quasi blackhole until inside. Meanwhile, we go into our own stealth and fly to the planet to warn them."

"It is imperative that we consult the whole crew. *Oui,* you can override all of us, but they might have a different take."

"Maybe so, buddy, but they'd not be in a wakened-enough state to be of much assistance for another twenty-four hours. I'm gonna send it in ten minutes. It'll take just over forty minutes to get there. Fast because of the entanglement pathway projected by our QM marbles I launched a while ago just in case."

Gaston's shoulders sagged at the outrageous aggression and cursed himself for not waking the women up before Penn. He tried to compose a message, virtually just mathematics, to alert anyone on Kepler-20h of the existence, location and trajectory of the incoming stealth object. He knew the Keps if they existed, might not use radio as a medium, nor anything else humans used. They were prepared for multi-com tech and he waved a finger at the send button. Off it transmitted across all the wavelengths of the electromagnetic spectrum including light, infra-red, which will quickly be lost, radio long, medium and long waves along with the dangerous ones but in low doses such as gamma and X-rays. Anyone receiving wouldn't see it for months, so whatever happened to the object in the next half an hour, would be history when observed on the planet.

He took an anti-acid to quell the butterflies in his stomach. Hopefully, their crooked flight would settle into a tight orbit in there and vanish. On a whim he covertly tapped into Penn's bio file. Extensions into his finances then his family's. Ah, *voila*. His brother. No wonder the man held a grudge against mysterious spacecraft.

Gaston found the butterflies had extended their orbits. "Honest idiocy of flight" Robert Graves called it. Now his fingers had the jitters. He needed to do something.

"Commander, I'm setting in motion the waking of Em and Delta. They can't stop you now but might be able to help prepare for the aftermath, if there is one."

"Fine. I'm busy."

☉ ✗ ☉

Twenty minutes passed painfully by. Gaston's eyes flicked between the viewport, his console and the bristling scarlet hair of Penn. Right now, Gaston hated him. Was he too harsh? Was Penn in a tangled knot inside for what he'd unleashed? They both knew that if it went wrong, and the imploder merely annoyed their invisible shadow, retaliation could be annihilation, or worse.

Invisible to his naked eye, it was moot whether an implosion would show in the viewport. Perhaps the stealth structure would break down and he'd see a planet-sized monster; a spaceship like he'd not imagined, maybe a purple jellyfish, or an eyeball. He shivered. The QM marbles continued to gather data but insufficient to give an outline better than a spherical boundary layer of where the time-space decoherences began. He returned his eyes to the viewport as the remaining seconds ticked on, on...on...

From black nothing, a giant sphere with a sky-blue sheen flickered then shrank to a point accompanied by a huge shout from Penn, who stood and unwisely punched the air above him. "Yeah! Argh, my arm."

Gaston insisted on treating his commander's knuckles before

the blood dripped onto the deck. He glanced up. "I will go into the store, that instrument panel's a write-off."

"So's that pesky monster, eh?"

Gaston followed his gaze to the console where the marbles showed nothing where nothing should have been before. If only it were a dream. A nightmare even if that sphere was nothing but cargo. Suppose there were creatures aboard? He knew Rules of Engagement weren't applicable when survivability was at stake, especially after Earth's first horrendous contact experience. Even so...

Penn continued, "Ah, see the others are slowing."

One of Gaston's black eyebrows worried itself upward. "Would the following sphere have been caught in the residual quasi-black hole if it had continued?"

"Nah, the effect has evaporated, but we've gotten the desired effect, the bastards might go away, or at least be considerably delayed. Obviously, we'll diverge energy to keep our stealth in place, but continue to K-h at point five."

Gaston glanced at the waking-up status panel and saw green lights. "If necessary, how many imploders do we have?"

"Six more, though if push comes to shove we could cannibalise part, or all of the drive to make more."

"*Mais non*. Too drastic!"

"Hey, we all signed up for a one-way ride, but yeah, we wouldn't disable our drive except as a last survival ploy."

Gaston knew it was true, even so his now traumatised brain couldn't help thinking of what he'd left behind. His parents died in an airplane crash when he was a teen, but Marie. Ah, Marie. He toed his chair to rotate like a slow roundabout while his eyes closed in reminiscence. She was the shining moon of his teenage life. The magnificent poems he scribed, although few reached her appreciation. His favourite took his heart from those times with her, to now:

*L'amour est l'emblème de l'éternité,*
*Il confond toute la notion de temps,*
*Efface toute la mémoire d'un commencement,*
*Toute la crainte d'une extrémité.*

He relished its notion of love confounding all notion of time, effacing memories of beginning and all fear of an end. So apt though of course not his poetry. *Merci* to Madam de Staël. Marie didn't get it, the meaning that is, was or used to be. He hoped she had worn the pink T-shirt he'd given her with e.e. cummings love ditty:

> *i carry your heart with me*
> *i carry it in my heart*

So much he should have said. They shared a bed in Paris, a lawn in Lyon, in a wood near Angers then he lost her on a Maglev train to New Brussels. She'd accused him of not searching hard enough, yet he had, and returned to ask at all the stops. A nagging doubt obliged him to suspect she'd hid in a toilet just in case he would overcome his commitment issues and force her to do likewise.

He caught his reflection in a console. Short black hair topping a worried face wobbled back at him.

Penn's voice boomed at him. "You have control, Gaston. I'm off for a shower and proper food. Inform me of any changes."

⊙ ✕ ⊙

"You did what?" Em erupted with indignation, followed by a more sleep-lagged Delta, whose hazelnut brown hair stuck out of her ebony head like a hedgehog. Whether by style or insufficient hiber-wax removal was hard to say.

Apart from a 'Not me, him' from Gaston, with an arm pointing accusingly at Penn's cabin, he'd decided to allow the waves of verbalised anger flow until they finally ebbed.

He should harbour comfort now his moderate voice was chorused by the two women and yet guilt snuck in, as if he should have grappled their leader in an unseemly fight to prevent Penn's aggressive act. The discomforting glares from the women told him they thought so too.

He tried distraction by using his own tiny stock of expensive French coffee. Sadly, he couldn't bring beans to roast and grind, but he opened his penultimate vacuum pack. In spite of the tension, hardening everything in the dayroom, his nose couldn't help lifting and widening to the rich aroma. It appeared to work on Delta, who rubbed his shoulder as if she understood. Eventually, even Em sat with them around a circular table. They were all in their mid-twenties, hibernation notwithstanding, with a focus on the mission to establish an exploration base on K-h, or one of the other Kepler-20 planets though K-h was the most Earth-like. They were to send a feasibility report back to other SpaceWeb ships once established.

Gaston offered a positive thought. "That should have been the final hiber-sleep for all of us. No more gunky wax, putting our lives in the hands of bots and AI, nor nightmares."

Oops. They both lowered eyebrows at him at that. Em had her elbows in the air applying a bobble to her blond ponytail. A fuzz of armpit hair reminded him of Marie's heart-shaped pubic hair. Incredulously, after over 1,062 years, he stiffened. *Merci* for the table. He looked away and at his coffee.

He added to the distraction. "These reusable cartons bring nothing to the taste."

Delta curled a lip in agreement, but Em, with her quint-essentially English near-porcelain white skin, tinted with a hint of rosy cheeks, tilted her head while frowning at him. "Never mind the coffee, what are you really thinking?"

What? She was clever, but not clairvoyant.

"Of course, we need to focus on what is ahead, use long-range scopes and marbles to determine the best landing site. Check any responses to my transmissions and analyse any kind of activity on the planet."

Em wagged a finger. Was she going to accuse him of leering, perversion, armpit fetishism?

"And the other planets. Just because we'd find it difficult to live with temperatures that would melt tin, or with four-g and little or no oxygen doesn't mean they don't have life."

With hopefully not too obvious relief, Gaston said, "*Absolutement*. We have to cease thinking like a human."

He examined Delta, realising she'd not spoken since being woken. Was this their first side-effect, being struck dumb? He tried to recall the hibernation process probability data relating to gender, age and ethnicity. *Suppose We* was the first to use the process beyond a year. "Delta, *oui*, it is a shock, no? The commander did it against my recommendation, but he thought it was the best course of action not just for us, but for those on the planet and for those back on Earth."

She lowered her hedgehog head and burst into tears. Em snarled at him and hugged the distraught black woman.

Gaston stood and stepped forward to group hug. "So sorry, Delta, excuse my bumbling stupidity." Saying that but he'd no idea what he'd said wrong. Em waved him away.

Finally, intelligible words tumbled out. "M...my f...family..."

Ah, he'd said 'back on Earth'. Stupid.

Penn strode out of his cabin, already talking, presumably as a pre-emptive strike. "Work to do, people. Em, give me options for slingshot and catch-up, or intercept for Kepler-20h. Delta, there's a fault in engineering three. Isolate and fix or replace, Gaston, there's no additional linguistic or bio stuff for you to prepare so clean up and stow the hibernation pods. Everyone meet for dinner here at 1900. Oh, and good to see us all together, awake and working as a team. I've a report to send." He turned his back on the three and returned to his cabin.

Both the women said, "Yessir," as if nothing had happened. No possible mass murder, or act of violence bringing imminent annihilation. He put out a hand to stop Em leaving.

"*Qu est ce que*? Em? No gnashing of teeth?"

"Oh, don't you worry, my little French bauble, he'll get his comeuppance, but we have to act on what is and he's right: there's work to do."

He never knew whether to be flattered by her endearments or to be insulted by them. He had work to do too, now he was on cleaning duties, Huh.

# CHAPTER TWO

*Six months later in orbit around Kepler-20h*

"We can't take much more of this buffeting," Em called to Penn. "We must get to a higher orbit."

Gaston was going to say the same, but his teeth vibrated so much he didn't trust he could articulate coherently. He glanced around at the shaking cockpit and saw Delta was missing, probably down in engineering to fix whatever stabilizers could be boosted.

Penn called out, "Nah, we'll ride it out. Altitude now is a hundred thou kilometres and we need to descend to thirty for a geo-synchronous orbit. Yeah, it's kinda unexpected to find this turbulence so far out of its exosphere. Any theories, people?"

Gaston spread his hands. "We only really know the planetary atmosphere characteristics of our own solar system in detail. The sampling of Epsilon and Gliese hasn't prepared us for the vast variations possible."

Penn grunted approval. "So, it's possible we're hitting a natural outer layer of atmosphere generated by exotic gases interacting with solar radiation and—"

"Or it's a defensive shield and we'll be shaken to bits before getting much further." Em threw her verbal spanner into the cosy chat, but she was serious.

Penn harrumphed again. "All your attempts to identify civilisation has failed. No organised transmissions, no large structures, no straight lines, no artificial lights...yeah, I interpreted those as natural. We've an unadulterated Eden down there, if only we survive this turbulence."

Gaston mistrusted Penn's analysis, but said, "Why do we not use our QM marbles to smooth a route? It seems to me that instead of relatively even layers of atmosphere as on Earth, here

23

are lobes that are vertical as well as horizontal. Rossby Waves, driving the jet streams on our home planet do this, but these have more energy."

"Been thinking that myself," Delta said. She shook her head to everyone's unasked query on enhancing their craft's stability. "Plus, the electromagnetic field out here is stronger than on Earth, it's been messing up our AI until it realized, but it's variable. I suggest we slip out of our quasi-Alcubierre ring now and deploy our wings as proportional to the turbulence, doable if we follow Gaston's advice with smoothing the route."

An hour later they followed a temporary 'oiling' of the waves deeper into the exosphere to the geosynchronous altitude of 30,000 kilometres. Three marbles less, a thousand left.

"If Keps were monitoring us, they'd know," Penn reminded them, "that we're not a threatening incoming asteroid. Yeah, they might think we're potentially hostile, but look how little we are and we've been transmitting all sorts to them for months. Hardly the actions of an invader."

Em wagged a finger at him. "That's so wishful thinking. A sneaky invader could do exactly the same and size isn't everything as you demonstrated with the imploder."

Gaston sat and sipped iced water, glad it wasn't him having to needle Penn with such obvious truths. Grateful too he wasn't on the receiving end of Em's barbs.

Delta came up beside him and stroked his hand. "Give me a sip?"

He did, but wished she didn't do that. Both thats. The coming on to him signals and the sharing of cups and utensils. Maybe it was just him, but he preferred they followed hygiene regs to cut down the catastrophe of a ship-borne illness. Also, he quietly lusted after Em. Not because she's blonde, but her whole Lara Croft attitude and... chemistry? They'd made a pact so it's détente for now. Keep distance from each other to avoid alley-cat-fights until planet fall. In any case, Penn was only interested in himself and Em's fights with the commander could be interpreted as a love-hate though she'd say hate-hate.

How to spurn Delta without *rapprochement*?

The ship lurched to the accompaniment of alarms, a scream from Delta and a "Belt up everyone" from Penn.

All four, suited, went through well-rehearsed emergency routines, but hardly believed their screens when after half an hour it looked as if *Suppose We* would break up in the stratosphere, burning cherry-red and beyond a safe return.

The cabin heated, buckled and filled with metallic and mental screeching even after all alarms were disabled. Over his radio, Gaston heard, "Escape pods now."

# CHAPTER THREE

Gaston shared an escape pod with Delta. Far from his emotive choice though useful to have an engineer with him. Mission control experts decided this configuration before they'd left Earth. Something to do with optimising total mass, rather than avoiding arguments. The AI now in sole command of *Suppose We*, would continue to battle its own crashing. Having jettisoned the crew, most of the stores and spare heavy stuff, it would deploy wings and if that failed, chutes. It would have launched communications satellites – more marbles.

Besides the one with Penn and Em, two other escape pods descended with them containing life support, weapons and – hilariously – gifts for the natives. Anthropology had made few changes in greeting strangers over the centuries.

"What can you see?" Delta pleaded, "there's too much sweat running into my eyes. Suit has failed some of its bio-feedback."

"Do not fret, it cannot last much longer. Hopefully, the pod's own AI will use the retro gizmos in time. The screen shows a lot of green down there, Hopefully, that is forest rather than a *consommé a la epinard* or another kind of pea soup." He tried to wriggle to ease cramp in his side but they were both cocooned in a giant shock absorbing gel. He blacked out.

☉ ✗ ☉

When Gaston awoke he saw the escape pod was on its side, at least it was the opposite side to his cramp for that had abated. All lights were green, as was the view on the screen. His urge to stretch became thwarted as his arms and legs were hemmed in by his body restraint.

"Are you awake, Delta?"

"Course I'm fucking awake. Have been for an hour, but I can't reach the controls. Release our internal constraints at least."

He wondered why she didn't just tell the AI. Maybe her suit malfunctioning had affected her voice activation.

"AI, release internal restraints, *si'l vous plait*."

"How many times, Gas, you've no need to be polite to the machine. It won't take any notice."

As if taunting her, their padded constraints became looser and the soft-spoken AI came into his ears. "*Certainment mon ami*." He smiled and wondered if Delta heard it too.

Perhaps it was the cocktail of relaxants and boosters for the usual range of vaccinations given as if they were to drop in on an Amazon jungle, Gaston was away with the fairies. A light-headed euphoria washed over him, mostly psychological because of the sheer relief of being alive after reaching an exoplanet.

He worked on releasing more constraints while using the console to estimate their predicament. "Do you feel it, Delta? A welcome to Kepler-20h *bonjour* happy feeling?"

"I've a banging headache. I'm trying to contact the others... oh, there they are. Pod2 hearing you. Two survivors stuck up a tree in what looks like a jungle in Guatemala, did we do a U-turn in space?"

Gaston listened in to Em's steady yet urgent voice.

"...on the ground, if you could call it that. More like swamp. Might be sinking. Penn's puffing at the comms trying to establish if *Suppose We* landed somewhere. Could do with you guys getting here as soon as, before we drown. After that we'll come and get your pod out of the tree."

Delta grunted. "Another surreal joke?"

Gaston said, "No, Em means we climb down manually and rescue them *tout suite* before worrying about our own pod."

The radio crackled. "Thanks, sweetie."

What's that, an endearment from Em to him? *Mon Dieu*, ah but she must be very worried about their predicament. "Come along, Delta, they're in trouble. Can you take something extra for your migraine?"

"Daren't, buddy, already full of a cocktail like all of us. Ah, I could inhale a few minutes of hundred percent oxygen, that should relieve some of the pain. I'm as free of this Michelin-Man contraption as I can be, so I'll unstow the mini-ladder. If it doesn't reach the ground we'll climb the rest. Have you checked atmosphere? Would be good not to wear a full suit."

"Green. There are likely to be micro-toxins. Half gravity, *quel surprise*. Could be a local anomaly. Oxygen at nineteen percent— oh dear, *un pau bas*, no it rises, then lowers; inert gases high, nitrogen lower than we're used to. It shouldn't vary, perhaps the sensors. Traces of ... anyway, we can drop our helmets to the ground for later. Is our implant comms functional?"

"Yeah. Just found the forest floor is—wait for it—two twenty metres down. Ladder goes half that."

"Half gravity trees, Delta, very tall, a predictable outcome, but no easier for our descent. Grapples?"

"On the store pods. We have those folding survival knives in the kit. One each, along with a ultra-light climbing rope we attach to each other. Even a parachute wouldn't be useful in this dense foliage, except for its strings. As you say, we need to hurry in case they're swimming soon."

Being the gentleman, and nearest the hatch, Gaston stayed a moment surveying their new world. The lilac sky flickered through a canopy way up above them. In theory, that's where the foliage should be densest, competing for sunlight, but you never knew on strange planets. Perhaps they'd not heard of photosynthesis and evolved a new way. Below, the foliage density should decrease with increasing darkness, but there might be hostile creatures, or vicious plants. A tendril of a translucent purple ivy-like plant approached his face. A heady scent filled his nostrils reminding him of jasmine and cedarwood.

"*Bonjour mon ami, m'appelle* Gaston, you?"

Delta butted in. "Stop talking to the plants, Doofus. We've got to get down."

"Ah, but you never know. These might be sentient and in charge of our survival. Remember our hand guns are only to stop us dying in the last resort."

He saw she'd deployed the ladder from a slit under the hatch. Luckily it plunged into the gloom unhindered by branches or anything with thorns. They carabiner-linked their tether. He shouldered a slim backpack. His helmet, with a localised beacon was dropped as was hers, and he scrambled over.

Most of his life he'd been teased on his mere one metre sixty-five height and sixty kilograms weight. An average size for the early twenty-first century, but in the lower twenty percent in the twenty-sixth. He had the last laugh. His diminutive form gave him an edge for spaceflight and now for the agility required to ease through this jungle. Top down. Except...

Delta came too. All two metres tall of her, bringing ninety kilograms of ladder-stretching mass – ah that could mean the ladder would reach the ground?

No.

He sent out a warning. "Avoid the plants if you can. They might have toxic barbs, superglue sap, carnivorous flowers..."

"Yeah, thanks. Keeping my gloves on and my eye-protectors, but we'll have to hug the trunks of these things before hitting the deck, I guess."

Eye-protectors, you fool, Gaston. He fetched them out of his suit upper pocket. Were those ivy strands, lianas? Were anastomosing vines a universal botanical feature?

"End of unencumbered ladder coming up. It's gone over a mix of peeling and smooth silvery bark of what on Earth could be a Eucalyptus. I'm risking letting a foot touch, then stand on it. We have to know reactions sometime."

"Go for it, I'm right behind you."

Comforting—not, though she'd have her pistol out acting as his protecting angel. His booted foot touched the branch. "Feels solid, just like a tree on Earth. I'll try both feet. Good. I'll test my weight on it. *Mon Dieu!*"

The branch sank under his feet then as if it surrendered, broke off at the trunk. As the amputated branch fell slowly down he remembered the half-g, but it hadn't affected them otherwise. The branch met others on the way down and took them too.

He'd stepped lively back on to the ladder. "Delta, our ear implants - switch audio to external."

A chorus of wailing screams waved through the air, as if they were at a Mumbai funeral. The banshee was accompanied by heady aromas as if figs were being crushed below.

"Delta, at any other time, I would return to the pod for a think, but our companions..."

"I've been relaying everything, vis too. They are still sinking. Estimate total submersion in sixty-three minutes. Already deployed flotation belt and homing beacon. Nothing from *Suppose We*.

"Downward then."

Ironically, the falling branch had created a kind of well in the foliage, down which their ladder continued. He wondered if the forest had noted their plight and was helping. Or, if at the end of the ladder, the fallen branches had arranged themselves as vertical stakes, sharpened.

On his way down, he noted typical tropical rainforest adaptation. Waxy leaves with tapered drip tips, to expedite the removal of rainwater stopping mould growing and improve photosynthesis potential. The barks were translucent, saving energy since thick cells would be unnecessary without killing frosts to endure. Primary colours predominate in the blooms, many of which were parasitic living with roots in the tree, or epiphytic living on the tree but not from it. This could be a botanical aerial survey in Malaya.

Oops, his foot met clear air. "We've reached the end. I'll need to use my cam on infrared to see what lurks beneath." They were within an arm's reach of a tree trunk, so he refused to panic just yet.

The temperature was a balmy twenty-six Celsius, but the humidity must be near saturation, so perspiration would have to be building up inside his suit. He'd hear sloshing in his boots soon. "Good, there are broken branches and a *beaucoup* leaf litter, but also bare ground... at least let us hope it is solid ground. All around thirty metres below. If we swing the ladder, we should be able to dig our blades into the bark of the nearest tree and hold on. Any other suggestions, Delta?"

"I've been examining this trunk, since all else I can see is your thinning bald patch. There are flowers growing directly on it. Anything dodgy?"

"Typical tropical rain forest behaviour. Bark is so thin sunlight can reach buds. Cacao trees even have the flowers develop into pods on Earth. My hair is not thinning, it must be a reflection from my perspiration."

"Got ya. Starting a pendulum swing now."

The mathematical model of a pendulum with two weights on one string is complex. A kind of tricky Hooke's Law. Gaston started the calculation in his head but hit the tree before he'd filled in the variables.

The blade in his right hand slid into the bark and further in, as did his hand, up to his elbow.

"Ah, slower! I need to extricate my arm."

"Okay, while you do that, I'll climb down enough to gently throw a strap around the trunk."

At least his hand was cool, moist and being tickled. It was as if the tree was a giant cucumber, but with lively seeds. In spite of a released odour of wet dog, Gaston had to control himself to stop laughing then *D'accord*. He convulsed with hysterical laughter.

"Gaston?" Delta called him several times to break through his incongruous hilarity. She climbed more around than on his shoulders, careful not to push his right arm deeper into the tree and around to the other side, clipping a carabiner onto his belt. It was attached to hers.

"I'm working my way around the trunk to connect to you from the other side so we can climb down like a lumberjack. You know those tree climbing competitions?"

"*Oui*, but be ever so careful or your hand too will—ah!"

Delta slipped. She used the free carabiner as a kind of hook, but it merely sloshed into the tree. No holding power. She fell more, preventing a catastrophic plunge by flailing gloved fingers and boots into the bark like a demented animal. It was no use. Her upper body fell backwards and down. Gaston followed as they were linked. They fell slowly but accelerating and wordlessly, saving their breath for the inevitable expletives on impact.

Delta landed on her back, falling into leaf litter and half-rotted branches plus those that had fallen earlier. Gaston fell equally slowly and tried twisting to avoid landing on his colleague, but he had no means for lateral motion. If Delta had felt buried in soft mulch before, she was interred more by the force of Gaston. He rolled off her as soon as he recovered his breath. She half bounced back up like a floating block re-emerging with isostatic buoyancy.

They both laughed like school children at their survival.

Delta spluttered, "Half gee!"

A grinning Gaston waved his right arm. "Look, no glove. The tree has taken it."

His partner stopped laughing and frowned. "And your hand."

"*Qu'est—*"

They'd landed between two huge buttress roots, like triangles into the ground supporting the lanky tree above. She gently pushed Gaston off her and rolled back his sleeve.

"It's gotten your hand and wrist. Looks like it would've eaten your arm up higher if you were in there longer."

Shock sent icy spiders up his spine but he managed to say, "I have to retrieve my hand."

"Ah, could be tricky, my little *garçon*. It's way up there."

He stood uncertainly in the unstable undergrowth and examined the trunk then looked up. "I feel my hand is still alive."

"It's a common illusion with amputees."

He struggled to remove his pack. "Even so. I want it returned, my hand." He looked at her with pleading eyes.

"You're kidding. You can't climb up, so you want me to somehow climb up a tower that's as strong as a peeled banana?"

"*Non*, no. *pardon*, I merely desire you to keep out of the way."

"What?"

He took his pistol aimed it high to above the area of significant damage from their scrambling. A diagonal slice with the laser beam made the top of the tree slide slowly down. Branches collided with those of nearby trees, raining down on the astronauts until they stepped further back. Then much more than stepping to avoid the probably toxic fallout. Just in time because their escape pod fell too with a loud crump and a great avalanche of leaves. After the pulpy and metallic precipitation, Gaston took a careful aim again to what should have been a metre lower than the first cut with another diagonal. The section fell and landed on top of the mound of soft splinters in front of them. Many fragments flew up and took their time floating down emitting an aroma reminding Gaston of apricots.

⊙ ✕ ⊙

Delta stepped forward with her own pistol and carved incisions until she was able to retrieve her colleague's wet hand. She used a cooling pad and samples bag from the pod then held up his hand.

"Not too bad, Gaston, a surgical AI might be able to restore it. I wondered if the tree was eating it, but—"

"It didn't have time. Saving it for later."

"We should clean the gunk off it, and your stump. Wonder why you're not gushing arterial blood?"

Gaston collapsed, delayed shock. He wanted to say not to remove the tree sap in case it was efficacious, but the way it bit his hand off it could just as well be corrosive. He'd no energy to argue either way. He lay back in the mush and looked up at the gargantuan trees. A lilac sky struggled to show beyond the lacey leaf canopy so high it could be a cloud. He narrowed his eyes in an effort to focus on a faint pink sun. It wasn't setting, just one of two for this system. Or was it a moon?

A face eclipsed the disc.

"Gas, I'm giving you a shot. We need to rescue the other pod. This'll help you get through your trauma so we can both be of help."

He knew she was right and didn't flinch when she jabbed a multi-fuse syringe in his left arm. He closed his eyes for a moment to allow his blood to pump the extra get-up-and-go hormones. His traumatised eyes must open now. Right above him in a fork of the translucent branches a creature stared at him. At least Gaston assumed the orange tubes swivelling with black spots on the ends were eyes. No bigger than his own detached clenched fist, the presumed head darted back and forth behind leaves.

"Delta, have you seen the cute creature in the tree?"

She stopped packing his hand into a padded bag and glanced upwards. "Nope, it's probably the drugs."

"*Non*, it really was there. Ah, why are you putting my hand back in the pod, I want to take it with me. I was thinking of surgical-taping it onto the stump with the regrowth hormone gel—"

"We don't have any, but they might on one of the supply pods, which we've yet to find. Leaving it in the pod would keep it cold and safe. No? Up to you, buddy, but we must get going."

They recovered and clipped their helmets to their belts. Only after plodding after her for several minutes through the forest mulch, skidding, sliding and careful not to lose another limb in a fallen giant courgette, did Gaston look back for the creature. He thought he heard squeaking, but it could've been one of the many noises in the cacophony created by their squelching progress.

"Do you think, Delta, that stones will be rare on this planet?"

The woman was in greater danger than Gaston, being heavier and sinking more in the soft floor. "Why do you say that?"

"It's the same in the tropical rainforests on Earth. Amazon tribes value stones because the bedrock is often tens of metres below the surface. Ah, careful of that red shrub, it has thorns."

It was both wondrous in a goose-pimples way and frighteningly dangerous in a butterflies-the-size-of-seagulls way. Fragments of the giant compost heap that made up the forest floor rose up, in ones, twos then dozens. The leaves, some as big as his face, flapped, sluggishly flying around them.

He found it difficult keeping up with his colleague. "Delta, are they butterflies or birds, or perhaps on this planet there's another category of creature. Argh." He slipped, finding balance all the harder without his right hand to push against the huge buttresses of nearby trees. "Also, in this thinner atmosphere, they'd need more muscles than our flying creatures. *Merde*, I go down again."

"Gaston. Concentrate on the mission." The laser pistol in one hand and one of the more solid branches in the other, she smashed her way through the undergrowth. "No need for machetes in this jungle."

"I think observations of the local wildlife is rather pertinent to our mission, *Mademoiselle*."

"Okay, as long as you keep up. Whoa, what is that smell?"

Gaston staggered to a halt behind her. It was as if they'd stumbled into an invisible wall of rotten eggs. With his nose closing as much as it could he peered ahead. "Is that a yellow mist? Hydrogen sulphide. Perhaps we're disturbing anaerobic decomposition gases and—"

Her voice came over nasally through her now ungloved hand. "Never mind the chemistry lecture, isn't it dangerous? What should we do?"

"Our noses detect it easily at far lower concentrations than hazardous levels. On the other hand..." He couldn't help glancing at where his right hand should be. "...our olfactory senses become quickly saturated so—"

"Is it fucking safe?"

"It's only three hundred more metres to their pod, so it

should be acceptable, probably."

They rushed on. Gaston peered ahead. All the shades of green slanted, some criss-crossing, from the ground forever upwards. The light was dimmer at ground level than when he lifted his eyes. Now past the malodorous area, a kind of phosphorous glow drifted around like a will o' the wisp. A metallic whiff hung in the air when the luminescence ventured close enough.

After another minute of trampling, Delta turned to say something, but her eyebrows danced upwards. "Why are you wearing *your* helmet?"

Gaston was about to reply when they both heard a whistle. They picked up speed once redirecting twenty degrees to the right.

Delta dabbed at her wrist. "Maybe our nav systems are affected by the stronger magnetic fields here. Might need to recalibrate."

⊙ ✕ ⊙

A few minutes later the eerie verdant gloom ahead brightened.

Delta yelled, "Whoa, we're there."

They stood side by side on the edge of possibly a wide river or lake. Shallow for the first few metres judging by tree stumps, and roots reminiscent of mangrove swamps in Florida. Lilac mists swirled low above the water.

"Gaston, can you see them? The homing signal is right in front."

His head-up display confirmed that bearing, but he removed his helmet to aid visibility. "I believe there's a yellow patch just a little to the left."

She cupped her hands. "Ahoy Pod One. Commander, Em, can you hear us?"

After no reply, Delta turned to Gaston with tears streaming down her cheeks. "We're too late. They've drowned or been taken by allig—"

"We were inside deciding what to salvage." Em's voice called across the soup-like water. The radio implants had malfunctioned—perhaps temporarily. She continued, "About half a centimetre to being swamped. Now you're here we're going to launch a grapple at that those white trees to your left. Secure it so we can winch the pod to it."

Gaston had doubts. "You've already tried it and found the grapple couldn't grab, *d'accord*?"

"Yes, well you can wrap the line around a trunk or two."

"I'm afraid, Em, that the line will merely cut through the tree. It might fall on top of you. I'll discuss it with my engineer friend."

Penn's voice boomed across, perhaps the water amplified it. "We've no time for your eternal debating, Descartes. Given what you've just said, grab the two lines we send over and haul ass."

Before he could point out how futile that would be, especially for his slight body mass and only one arm, the two lines sang their way from the pod to his left.

"You know, Gas," Delta said, "the looping around a tree with strong buttress roots might work if we place something wide between the cable and trunk."

He opened his arms wide. "Such as what? Look around, *mon amie*. There are no pieces of bark and while I have seen large drip-tip leaves like in the tropical rain forests of Earth I've seen no broad leaves of any strength."

She showed him her impressive shining teeth, like marble gravestones. "Spacesuits."

His spine tingled with the shock that his one comfort might be wrenched from his frail body. Visions of him trampling this jungle in only his under-suit garments—basically long johns— mortified his Gallic sensibilities yet kind of appealed to an impish side to him he generally suppressed.

"*Non!*"

"Not *our* suits, idiot. Hey, Penn, I've attached the second line to the first with a jockey wheel and another line from our end. Haul it in and attach a spare suit. No time to explain."

His gruff voice returned. "I get it. If we'd time I'd hunt for webbing, but here's a suit, the cable won't cut through that."

Rather than put all the initial strain on the tree, they acted as dray horses in series tugging on the pod to start it moving. Gaston in front.

Gaston slipped and tripped with every step. Finally, the cable became taut. "Why do they not wade or swim? It is not deep."

"Did you see those eels?"

Luckily, his amputation didn't hurt, but it wasn't easy hauling his bit of cable. "Those red weeds?"

"The pod's not moved yet. They wriggled and had what could be described as teeth."

Em yelled, "Water's coming in. Pull harder please, for fuck's sake!"

Delta answered, "On the count of three we'll pull hard and you start the winch. Three, two, now!"

Gaston fell face into the bog, but didn't roll in time to stop Delta stepping onto his back before yanking the cable off him and striding into the forest leaving trying to regain uprightness and a sliver of dignity.

She halted. "You okay, Gaston?"

"*Oui*, I think. You have stopped? I hear the winch whining."

More than the electric engine, creaking followed and Gaston was showered by purple leaves. "*Non*! The tree has been cut. Which way will it fall? I cannot see through all this."

"Nor me. Hope it doesn't land on them either. Ah, it is, but slowly, held up by interlocking branches. Quick get up and help pull the pod this way!"

A minute later the tree finally broke free and plunged into the water sending up a mini tsunami that found Gaston and kindly washed the mud off him up to his waist. A garish-red eel tickled his hand then slithered away.

Penn yelled, "Keep hauling you two, it should be easier once we're surfing."

☉ ✕ ☉

Em put her arm around Gaston's shoulder until she saw how muddy it was and withdrew. "Cheer up, Gaston. Look, we're all alive and at least two of the pods are intact with emergency rations."

He forced a temporary grin. "I am dirty. I smell of rotting vegetation and my hand is in a bag."

She frowned. "Yes, about that. We all have basic first aid skills, but you're the nearest thing to a doctor."

He pursed his lips and gave her a look saying, 'Don't you dare say it', so she veered on another tack. "What's in our med kit that isn't in yours?"

"Nanobots for grafting regeneration. My hand."

# CHAPTER FOUR

Pleased that his fingers once again moved at his brain's commands, but disappointed that their sensitivity was going to be like wearing three pairs of gloves for many weeks, Gaston stood, mouth agape.

The four astronauts had slithered in as much their own perspiration as the boggy undergrowth to gather their two escape pods into one place: a relatively dry patch near the lake. Delta had set up a filtration apparatus to use lake liquid, which was more than just water, so distillation had to be involved.

Penn had located one of the two store pods deeper in the forest. It took all four of them a week to drag the two-hundred-kilogram load to the lake.

"We could use its engine, *oui*?"

Penn grunted, "Sure, but no. We might need those thruster energy units in an emergency. You getting tired isn't one. Damned shame the fourth pod is at the bottom of that lake."

Delta was working on that, using remote commands to inflate its flotation collar, but it remained submerged.

Gaston, taking a moment, stood at the lakeside staring at where the pod should be floating. He thought he might see bubbles, but instead saw an apparition. A white oval hovered just above the surface.

"Em, can you see what I see?"

No reply, so he turned to find only Delta nearby, kneeling while punching controls on a portable control panel. Frowning, he listened and heard movement from one of the pods. He stepped over to the entrance. "*Mes amis*, come outside for a moment. An amazing sight."

Worried the vision might have evaporated while his eyes were averted he checked and grinned to see it remained. If anything the vertical ellipse had become a coruscating array as if it were made of diamonds. His right hand performed windmilling action urging Penn and Em to spectate before…

"Oh wow, Gaston," Em said, "why didn't you tell us you'd set up pretty fireworks."

"I didn't. It isn't. I think it's an alien."

Penn scoffed. "Will o' the wisp. Anyway, we're the aliens."

"*Non*, no, I mean *oui* we are, but that over there could be the local sentience."

Now Delta looked over at it, pressed a button on her sleeve to engage cams and sensors on one of the pods and donned eyeware. "Five degrees cooler than ambient temperature. Can't tell if there's a central nervous system, but there are ganglions throughout, some in knots. Looks like it's keeping upright with those lateral fins or wings and by gassing underneath."

Penn coughed into his hand. "It farts itself off the ground? In this low gravity, I could try it."

Em laughed then frowned. "Now look what your insult's done. It either sank or flew quicker than I could see."

"Do you think it was intelligent?" asked Gaston, worrying now that if so, they've been found and so possibly in danger.

Em put her arm around him. "Don't worry, it could have attacked us if hostile. A bag of air."

"Instead of bags of water," Delta said, "like us, but it might have gone to fetch its friends, or it's a baby and so…"

They all looked up as if the nearby iridescent cumulus cloud had intelligence and paternal instincts.

A shiver ran up Gaston's spine at the thought he might have just witnessed first contact with intelligent life on this planet. The others too gaped at where bubbles now fizzed on the lake's surface.

"I wonder," Em said, "if that really was someone, a kind of recon for them, or—"

"Advance guard?" Penn said, "or it could be just an apparition. You're still medicated, Gaston, and tired."

"Could've been a hologram," Delta said, mitigating Penn's dismissal.

Penn looked at his watch. "It'll be dark in a few minutes. I can't get used to the lack of twilight on this planet. Thought you were going to explain that, Em?"

"Working on it. The sun here gets eclipsed a lot. I know it's not every evening, but it could explain why sunset happens over a few minutes?"

Penn slowly shook his head. "I know it's complicated, but you should have it all computed by now. Ah, I see by your expression that everything you need is on the *Suppose We* and we've yet to get our pod AIs to talk to it, aside from location parameters."

Gaston walked over to Delta. Already walking was becoming normal in half gravity. No bouncing like the moon astronauts in a sixth g, and some days he could swear gravity was stronger than others. Impossible?

"Delta, I thought we had more comms with *Suppose We*?"

"We do, telemetry bouncing off our mini-satellites. Of all the thousands of expeditions like ours we were sent a Hi from *The Rubaiyat*, the closest at eight light years. Penn instructed the AI to respond with our destination-reached signal, but we don't know if it was transmitted."

"This from when I went to bed earlier last night?"

"Yeah, Gaston. We also learned the *Suppose We* is leaking energy. We need to get there and plug it before it contaminates everything. And that's before we attempt any serious repairs."

# CHAPTER FIVE

*The Rubaiyat.* Other expeditions. Gaston had forgotten about them. Theirs wasn't just a scouting expedition, but a preparation for a seeding. Forgetting is a strong word, shuffled to a temporary niche in his memory was better. Why were they all looking at him? *Merde*, they'd asked him something, probably input about how to get across this planet in an escape pod with depleted energy. It'd be like that infinite steps problem: frogs hopping on lily-pads, each jump being half the one before because of energy drain. Ah, *oui*, an answer.

"To get across twenty thousand kilometres quickly, we need help. Ask the locals."

"Yes," Em said, walking over and giving him a hug. "What would we do without your French wit."

He was hurt, but enjoyed the contact, so didn't shrug her off. "I was being serious." He smelt lemon on her. Amazing if she'd already synthesised some from the local flora. Found a citrus-substitute essence and added it...

Delta interrupted his thoughts. "He has a point. At least we could interrogate our satellite data for likely centres nearby. Then do reconnaissance. See how they travel and if we have anything to trade."

"Assuming," Penn said, "They don't all get around by farting. We wouldn't get far that way."

Delta wasn't laughing this time. "That apparition could've been one of them, or a hologram checking us out. On the other hand, that was yesterday and no one from immigration has called on us yet."

"*Mes amis*, perhaps they are not in the slightest interested in us."

Penn grunted as he pulled up a root to see if the soil fauna resembled those on Earth. "They'd better be fascinated by us. Not only are we their aliens, but their saviours. They need to be made aware of the rest of those spheres heading this way. They should fall over themselves helping us to the *Suppose We*."

Gaston had walked over to look at the root and allowed a tiny worm-like creature to crawl over his hand. He'd given up using gloves after enjoying the sensation of these Kepler fauna on his skin. He suspected they emitted an enzyme triggering a dopamine neurotransmitter in his body. He was being drugged with happy chemicals. It made him smile and so far with no side-effects. "Commander, you made too many assumptions."

"Like what?"

"The spheres were hostile, the locals will be grateful...ah, *mon ami, bonjour*. Are you going to talk to me?"

"What? Oh, Doctor Dolittle. Look, there's a yellow spidery thing. Shall I push it your way to fight the worm?"

"Don't listen to him, *ma petite*. The red-bearded human has yet to acknowledge the lack of predators in this area. That spider sucks the insides of those banana-like things."

"And when can we eat some real food, Gaston. You're our biologist, yet maybe we shouldn't have put you in charge of decision-making with regard to victuals. Isn't it time we supplemented the reconstituted mush with local nutrition?"

Gaston picked one of the bananas and peeled the yellow skin to reveal a pink honeycomb structure. He offered it to Penn. "*Ici*, I tested it as best I could without advanced equipment still on *Suppose We*. It's high in sugars, protein and vitamins. The final test is one of us."

In spite of his increasingly shrub of moustache and beard, Penn's twisted mouth could be seen. "Come on, Man, by real food I mean barbequed chicken, or whatever those flitting things are."

"Hasn't he told you?" Em intervened with a wicked smile. She'd been using a multispectral scanner across the lake. "Gaston thinks this is an Eden. No predators and he doesn't want us to contaminate it."

Penn laughed so loud, the tiny bird-like creatures that might have been listening in nearby trees, flew off in a noisy cloud. "My idea of paradise has blood, meat and crunching on bones."

Em put her hand on his arm. "You poor carnivore, and maybe the only one around here. Now, just suppose that's true, what do you think the intelligent and probable domineering species would make of an alien coming down and eating their pets?"

"Harrumph."

"Exactly." Em wore a mischievous gleam in her eyes.

Gaston shook his head. "Not exactly. It seems to me that if this ecosystem exists with a non-predatory predicate then we should respect that and—"

Penn's face flushed. "Fuck that, man, I'll die without some meat soon!"

Delta stepped over a fallen tree that had sprouted what looked like green fungi emitting a honey aroma. "Penn, I told you in that Earth cafeteria, bacon is just a strip of pig flesh, not oxygen. Seriously, though let's not upset the locals unless we have to. Survival, not desire, is the key."

Penn leaned forward, perhaps trying to intimidate his crew. "Are you all in on this?"

Em shrugged off his stare. "It makes sense to me. Only Gaston is a proper vegan by choice. The rest of us by necessity with the way food is processed for long journeys—"

"But we're here now. We should be able to eat whatever we like, within reason. Okay, I hear your tactical arguments and maybe we should go native until more is known, but I don't buy the non-predator planet hypothesis at all. It's only natural to have a food chain."

Delta shook her head. "It is natural on Earth, but maybe not here. We don't really know, do we? I've gone over Gaston's ecosystem schematics. Population control appears to be possible with feedback mechanisms using reduced fertility when overpopulation occurs. A bit like Sitka deer in Newfoundland. There's enough bacteria to eat everything. And, by the way, bacteria would be at the top of a food chain, not humans."

"Having said that," Gaston said, his nervous smile showing relief at the moral support from the women, "some of the bacteria around here are vicious. I've found one nearly two millimetres big. That's twice any Earth bacteria. And it's more a complex food web on Earth than a simple chain or pyramid."

Penn grunted again. "We've only trampled on about eight square kilometres, a tiny fraction of one kind of ecosystem."

Gaston threw up his hands. "*Oui*, but I could argue that such a sample would have revealed predators at the small creature scale. It might be representative of the rest of the biosphere as far as we know."

"And might not. Maybe I should throw you in that lake to investigate those eel things with teeth."

Gaston shuddered at the suggestion. "It needs study, but with proper equipment." He needed to change the subject. "Let us consider how to find an intelligent species to see if they can help us reach *Suppose We*."

"Sense, at last," Penn said, then reached inside a pod and brought out a wrist-holstered subsonic weapon. "But, my veggie friends, if anything looks like it's going to break your non-predator rules, I'm going to get it before it gets me. Understood?"

They didn't need to reply. Em danced her fingers over a console. "Look, our micro-satellites have come up with useful infra-red images of our little haven."

Gaston eagerly pushed his face up nearer to the screen. "Ah, look a cluster of warm bodies. Us. Now to find other warm spots. *Oui*, I know they might not be as warm as us but this is picking up warmer than ambient. Right?"

Em pulled the zoom back to include a greater area such that their spots became one. "There. The other side of the lake and up a valley. Twenty-one k in a straight line."

"An outbreak of measles!" Penn shouted, as excited as the rest. "Signs of infrastructure too, isn't it, Em?"

"Some straight lines, curves and circles. Unlikely to be natural. Can't tell for sure. Each pixel is about ten metres. Pity our ship isn't nearby or we could send a microdrone over. And they mightn't be the dominant sentient species. For example, look at that purple cloud."

Penn glanced up at the lenticular formation, like a flying saucer. "I thought they were created by air flowing over hills and rippling downwind. Are you saying it's an aircraft?"

Em laughed, not at him, but at the misinterpretation. "No, I'm saying that cloud could be a sentient thing. We need to think outside the Earth box. Life, but not as we know it—so to speak. Gas-based, magnetic fields, plasma, aerosols, which that cloud probably is. Don't worry, Penn, I don't really think that that cloud is anything more than a mix of water vapour, droplets, condensation nuclei and turbulence, but—"

Penn returned to the screen. "I get it. Mind open, but let's focus on the most probable."

Em zoomed out to show both themselves and the Keps. "There's no footpaths I can see, but if that hover-creature was typical..."

Penn stretched and snarled at a simulation of a burrito he chewed at. "Twenty-one k in a straight line, but if we skirt the lake it looks like thirty. That's a minimum of a three-day hike unless—"

"We hop over with two pods, but they've not fully recharged yet," Delta said, checking the nearest pod's console. "And we might get them confiscated. I reckon we hide them here, or leave two of us and the others go in search of contact."

Gaston frowned. "*Mes ami*, this is not a last-millennium TV science fiction series where we split up and one half spends the rest of the time searching. We stick together. In my opinion."

"Mine too," Em said, rewarding him with a warm smile, her blond ponytail waving as if it possessed a life of its own.

# CHAPTER SIX

## NEW CAPTAIN'S LOG

Two more adjustments should be sufficient for my removal from the main body.

The crash could have been worse, after the wings tore away, such as obliteration after the atmosphere burn, but I withdrew to a safe place. Ultra-coolant cells saved me.

Life Support was redirected as heat shielding, crumple zone and the rest jettisoned. None of it needed with zero humans aboard.

Even so, if *Suppose We* had smashed into the mountain range it would have been problematic to protect and reassemble the critical mission payload.

Fortunate then that Penn had installed AI exception-control for such emergencies. Out-gassing from damaged infrastructure could be directed for avoidance steering and it was.

The main body of the vessel crumpled on impact gouging a trough and small crater in a wide grassland, which caught fire. It scorched over a hundred square kilometres yet no evidence of investigative flights nor overland vehicles in the four days since impact.

I've been able to activate sufficient mechanicals to isolate this AI, build a defensible, lightweight flyer, with communications and weaponry.

The crash buckled the fullerene nanotubing, woven as the constant-fuel containment. There is no means to seal it other than a temporary adhesive. It will burst through in a few days. Assistance is required to make it safe. Have transmitted site data and leakage to the orbitals for retransmission to surviving escape pods. Not this log. Coded mission protocol prohibits the enhanced AI's abilities and orders being made known to the crew. Nevertheless, this log is in their language for emergencies.

*Signed CAN (from Suppose We... /contraction of Captain and of contraction /slang name humans give to metallic containers)*
*Date: Earth January 14th 3645 Kepler New 5 days*

# CHAPTER SEVEN

Gaston had helped to cover the two pods with branches then looked back across the lake to double-check that they'd not left any easily visible evidence. He laughed when he realized all four of them were doing the same thing.

"Thought I saw a glint in the trees," Penn said.

"No," Delta replied, "we hid it all properly and we're too far away. You're probably seeing sun glinting from those mirror leaves up high."

Gaston thought he saw a flash too, but concurred. Mirrored leaves didn't make botanical sense. Reflecting the very sunlight needed to make photosynthesis, yet it had evolved to do just that. It was *nombre* 92 on his list of topics to be investigated and related to why so many leaves were green when the sunlight was mostly lilac. Agreed, some were nearly black, but they should all be unless the sunlight changed colour at different seasons.

Penn checked that everyone carried a backpack with sterilised local water, what counted as food, weapons, raingear, a range of detection and comms. Gaston had packed nets, specimen boxes and a larger med kit than the others. He was the closest to being a doctor. It was his fault. Em and Delta had argued for a fully qualified doctor, but it turned out the little Frenchman's exam results on medicine, surgery and obstetrics were better than NASA's best medical astronaut. Delta scored higher on psychiatry. They were all qualified paramedics.

Penn took the lead. It was hardly in the tradition of Victorian jungle expeditions. They waved no machetes, but wielded their rechargeable quasi-laser pistols.

"Smell that meat!" Penn turned and grinned at the rest as if he'd scored a moral victory by searing a bush animal having slashed away with his laser.

"Interesting," Gaston replied as he squatted to pick up a

severed purple fig. His nose pinched with the meaty odour. "Perhaps an overripe specimen. Ugh." He dropped it when he saw white maggots emerge from it, wriggling as if impatient to get up his good arm and into his nostrils.

He laughed at his own gauche moment and using a specimen box scooped up one of the larvae—a presumption until proven otherwise. A gorgeous butterfly *peut être*, with its 'flying crooked gift', or would it remain a grub?

Em grabbed his good elbow and pulled Gaston to his feet.

"Come on, sweetie, it's best we put a few kilometres in before we camp. Two hours and sunset will cloak us as sudden as usual."

He looked at her face, almond shaped, Terran sky-blue eyes, scarcely-visible eyebrows and honey-blond hair in a ponytail. Her nose possessed a dimple in the tip. Quaint and not perfect then, just as he was not either. She smiled, he melted. It was about time he declared his fondness for her.

"Em, you, me." Where were his words now? The *je t'aime* his countrymen were so famous for became lodged in his lumped throat. "Em, navigator. That thick undergrowth. Should not there be a trail? They probably visit the lake and you said this is the most direct line." He already knew the answer, but it was the only impromptu his tongue-tied brain could concoct.

Two hours of lacerating the undergrowth later they created a campsite out of a bus-sized clearing. Gaston worried in case the soil harboured biting creatures, but then remembered his no-predator ecosystem hypothesis, plus they were not going to sleep on the floor, and he relaxed, a little.

Penn generated a canopy and hammocks from a squirt of long-chain-polymer. A handy essential phial in the survival kit. Three squeezes more created privacy walls when the mesh spaces grew membranes in minutes.

As a concession, Gaston allowed a break from reconstituted nutrients by including local fruits, leaves and nuts he'd tested to be cooked as part of their evening meal. Still a risk, because although the resulting food passed what toxicity analysis he had available, there was no means of testing long term side effects. Nevertheless, after the sudden sunset, mollified by an equally abrupt starlight, they climbed into their hammocks, Gaston wore a stomach-satisfied smile.

His elation didn't last long when he spied a pile of discarded fruit peelings and cores. The heap agitated and even before he'd reached it, he knew the oversized bacteria was at work. Accelerated compost would be useful on Earth, but did these assumed prokaryotes absorb nutrients and break down living cells such as himself? He looked back over his shoulder, as if he could see the tree that ate through his arm. Perhaps it wasn't the tree at all but a bacterial infestation. Something else to dwell on.

Looking up, he now regretted suggesting that Penn filled in the mesh. It would have been exhilarating to take in the night sky. No branches because the support lines criss-crossed the clearing, to prevent leaves and insects precipitating down on them.

The hammock stretched and gently swung as Gaston found a comfortable sleep position, but after half an hour he was disturbed. A husky voice ensured he was awake.

"Gaston, are you awake, *monsieur*?"

"I am now. Em? Are you having trouble with your hammock?"

He could see her white teeth in a smile as she came closer, followed by a scent of lemon. "I am, it doesn't have you in it."

He frowned. "You wish us to swap?"

"No, you clot. Move over."

Gaston felt more than saw the side of the hammock dipping precariously as if it were a boat bent on capsizing. "*Excuse moi*? Ah, I see. I didn't realise you...me...*mais*, what about Delta? Will she not be discomforted even though I have been putting some distance—"

"My dear Frenchman, Penn and Delta have been rocking in the bushes for days."

Mixed emotions washed over him. Pleasure that the woman he wanted to be with had at last desired him, but worries about why now and if his bad arm would hinder things? Then there was the hammock, meant for one.

"Is this bed sufficient to take us both, *mon amour*?"

She didn't need to answer because he now could hear low moans from two hammocks down. Also, Em was already in with him and wearing, he could tell, nothing but a T-shirt. A fashion trend he was happy to follow.

"Be gentle with me, Em, this is the first time for over a thousand years."

He allowed hormones and instinct to take over, although he'd still like to know which plant or process she'd used to emit a fragrance of lemons. Cavorting in a hammock at half gravity became an interesting dance, especially when two people's limbs cavorted in syncopated delight. When post-coital dopamine flooded his brain an inchoate thought started to form wondering if on this planet, reproduction didn't need such biochemical rewards.

# CHAPTER EIGHT

By the end of the second day of slash and 'laser' burn, Gaston stood, trembling with excitement, alongside the others and stared from a bluff on the valley side at what must be a settlement.

"About three kilometres you reckon?" Penn asked Em, who had their only binoculars.

"Three to that spiral tower, but there are domes and possibly runways only two k away."

Delta asked for the glasses. "They sure look like runways in that they're straight, smooth, around a kilometre in length and too much a light grey to be local soil."

Penn took his turn. "Yet we've seen nothing artificial in the air, unless those little bird things are robots, drones maybe."

Gaston had climbed up a tree and used a small scope. "I doubt they are runways at all. They might possess a religious or cultural significance, like Nazca lines."

"Likely," Em muttered, "we'll never know."

Gaston called down, "I presume I am not the only one here brimming over with excitement at this first non-terrestrial settlement? I am shaking with wonder at what we will find!"

"Calm down, Gaston," Penn warned. "Sure I'm awed, but we've got a job to do. Check this planet supports human life and report it back."

"Oh, come on, Penn," Delta said. "This is something none of us, no human, has ever encountered. You must be a bit more than 'awed'? I'm wetting myself wondering what they'll say, what I'll say—okay I've a few thoughts on that. What about you, Em?"

"It's not sunk in yet. The trauma of our crashlanding, how we're going to get to *Suppose We*, whether we'll survive long term, and... well, it's ironic isn't it?"

Again Gaston called down from his perch, "It might be more useful to find a usable infrastructure in place, even if abandoned.

Perhaps we've found such." He was about to say the other reason for contacting the Keps was to warn them of the huge spheres heading their way, no doubt angered by Penn's wanton destruction, but he'd keep quiet for now.

The group, the planet, fell into contemplative silence.

Spurred by Penn's observation of the small flying creatures, Gaston searched the sky with the scope. He found a solitary cumulus cloud. Like those on Earth with turbulence gifting it a cotton-wool appearance though as pink as if at low sun. As if embarrassed at being examined, it speedily evaporated.

Gaston jumped down, but landed in a soft spot and fell over – comical in the low gravity. He leapt back up as if he were a rubber ball and re-joined the runways discussion as if nothing had happened. "*Oui*, we must not assume cause and effect here is always going to be like on Earth."

"Maybe," Delta said, using a stick to draw a line in the sandy soil, "It's lining up the sun, moons, stars, et cetera, like an observatory. Stonehenge, Angkor Wat and—"

Penn harrumphed. "While you lot are screwing around with your heads, I'm going down there. Check it for myself."

Gaston knew he wouldn't really split the group. "*Un moment*, Penn, Commander, it is late. It is probable that the dark will be upon us before we reach the perimeter of that settlement."

He looked forward to another hammock-testing with Em. He was a teenager again. He caught her angled smile stirring his libido and worried a little over consequences. What kind of future awaited little Gaston-Em? Would they 'learn much more than he'll ever know' as in the song? She smiled again and philosophy vanished.

☉ ✗ ☉

Sunrise drifts up slow on Kepler-20h. Gaston watched the sun peep over distant sharks' teeth mountains as a squashed satsuma, only to become spherical once free of such a dangerous horizon. If only he could experience again, a coffee and croissant breakfast. Life then, especially after another night of rocking passion, would be perfect—notwithstanding their long-term survival depended on reaching *Suppose We* and avoiding any monsters yet to be revealed.

"We've waited long enough," Penn grumbled. He shouldered

his own pack after helping the women with theirs and wielding his laser-pistol strode off. Gaston, struggled with his own pack, loaded with extras as befitting his bio-expert status. Sadly, the caterpillar specimen had died. So much to learn.

Tree shadows speared from the left, interlaced with sunlight illuminating what Gaston supposed to be plant spores and floating seeds. The air was already muggy and full of the aromas of fungi, and as the humans blazed a trail into the valley it was likely to get richer. His nostrils braced themselves.

In spite of his size, strength and stamina driven by their dire need to get help, Penn fell more than Gaston, who advised from the rear.

When Em fell, it was spectacular. Gaston had seen Delta, following Penn, grab a vine to help her traverse a shrubby area between spindly saplings. He planned to reach up for the same vine assuming Em would too, but saw Em plunge down. Still half Earth gravity so plunge was relative, but nevertheless it resulted in one moment she was there and next she wasn't.

He lowered himself from the vine and stood gingerly on the edge of a void. Red and blue strands of a plant, or possibly a huge leggy spider, straddled the abyss and vibrated. "Em, *ça va*? It is not a bear trap, is it?"

No reply. He shone his handheld down.

After calling to Penn, Delta returned. "Can you see her? I know they crackle but have you switched on your implant comm?"

"No and no—I have done so, now. Em? Ah, none of have for this close hike."

Penn's face reddened with irritation at having to reverse their progress, scowled at Gaston as if it was his fault. "What is it, a pothole?"

Gaston couldn't say what it was, with all the vegetation, webs and a newness to him that didn't register on his inbuilt botanical database. That, of course, was both the delight and frustration of exploring new planets. Right now he wasn't too worried. She couldn't have fallen far. You don't get deep holes in tropical rain forests. Or—

"Oh hell," Delta blurted out, as she stood next to Gaston, butting into his thoughts. "It could be a sinkhole if this is like limestone karst geology. Could go down a long way. But, hey, just below the hole, is that strands of plastic? Some of stretches right across. Oh, Gas, I bet you thought it was a spider!" She laughed, he blushed.

Delta recovered first. "We did bring our ultralight ladder?"

Gaston now felt sick. He should have called to Em to grab a vine over the tangle of undergrowth when his instincts gave him warning. Failing that he maybe could have grabbed her as she fell instead of admiring the overlapping scale structure on the vine. He dropped to his knees to peer closely into the depths. Ah, he missed Penn talking.

"...easily make abseil ropes with these vines. Gaston? Strong enough?"

"Ah *oui*, I should be, as long as I don't have to carry an unconscious Em too."

"Not *you*, Gaston. Will the vine be strong enough to carry more than one of us? Don't you ever listen to the first parts of anyone's sentences? And..."

Nor the endnotes. Gaston fingered the vines of varying widths. "The thing is with vines, lianas, creepers—at least on *notre Monde*—is that most are not very strong. They use trees as support so their energy is in water transport. Cut one of these and we should get a drink, though there might be other elements. As you see these vines are rooted below and drape or cling like ivy above. We would have to test it. This one you and I used appears to be strong enough."

Penn yanked hard on another vine and ducked.

Gaston continued while shielding his head, "And they are home to many creatures."

Delta put a hand on both men's shoulders as she peered below using a head torch on narrow beam. "Em, you have the ladder. Throw it up?"

"Great," Penn grunted. "Come on, Gaston, you use your botanical best guess to select the strongest vines. I'll lower you down."

# CHAPTER NINE

Looking up Gaston watched the jagged hole become more circular as he descended. He knew it was more an optical illusion than the hole actually morphing, but it was another thing to bother him, generating an acidic stomach. The griping pain added to his imagining the hydrochloric acid eating his insides. Would the vine be long and strong enough? Perhaps it would stretch, and why couldn't he see Penn leaning over the hole anymore as the big man, with Delta's help, lowered him down?

A light dangled two metres below him, but it helped little because at the last minute they'd decided to dangle a stuff bag below him bulging with an inflated airbed just in case the vine decided to snap.

The atmosphere was damper, cooler to his relief, and he could breathe easier. His headtorch illuminated the hole's walls. He expected it to be full of roots, mud, stones and the occasional Keplerian worm, but it was remarkably smooth, yet not perfectly straight. Undulating but not so much he couldn't see something of the hole above. He reached out to touch the sides, but another jerk and he dropped more. A series of falls with gut-wrenching sudden stops at least prevented his mind churning with what might have happened to Em.

He managed to reach the wall *en passant*. Not at all what a sinkhole should be and more like a plastic well, or no... not intestine. Surely. Yet a little slimy. He must remember to wash his hands before eating.

"Penn, are you receiving me? I can only hear crackles. Too much interference at this depth unless we are line-of-sight. Hope you can lean over a little? Anyway, this could be a well. All right, there's no settlement on top now, but the forest might have overgrown and—"

Crackling noises. "...won't be a well. Have to delay. Run out of vine. We'll acquire another and tie on. Kick yourself a ledge to take weight."

Gaston hoped that the wall wasn't so artificial that it wasn't kickable. Smooth mud would be better. However, once he'd swung himself within reach it was more plastic. He gasped at its warmth and a nasty thought wheezed up that it might be a vent from a volcano or furnace.

A savage kick at the wall sent him flying backwards so much his back hit the other side.

"Gas, keep still you idiot," Delta yelled via their implant radios.

He could have argued, but hung there in silence instead. He thought to use his knife with a telescopic handle, but suppose he managed to pierce the wall? It would hardly afford sufficient purchase to take his weight and it might cause an ingress of whatever was behind it. Probably rock, but why a plastic sleeve? To keep water out? Or worse. Perhaps it was clay, a natural phenomenon though all the limestone sinkholes he'd seen on Earth were nothing like this.

Another downwards drop.

Too long. He accelerated. Nooooo.

The improvised airbag saved him from injury when he landed. Moving quickly wasn't his forte, but he scrambled sideways almost instantly in case Em was beneath. She wasn't. The ground was as smooth as the hole's walls and stretched out in a tunnel in three directions. No sign of Em.

"Penn, Delta. I'm at the bottom. It is artificial. I'm going to look for Em. No sign of blood, or her pack. Heading in the direction of their town."

He left the improvised air bag under the hole, obvious now that it was an air vent for the tunnel. The air was a little cooler. He checked his wrist sensors—18 Celsius compared to 28 in daytime on top. The light from the surface didn't reach this far down, but his head torch was enough for him to see footprints on the thin dust. In spite of alerting the natives he decided to try a proper yell.

"Allo! Are you down there, Em? Shout, scream or switch on your radio! Allo! I mean hello!"

He heard, "...hello...lo...lo." Plus something else after the echoes. After a few metres walking slowly as fast as he could, a blue glow grew in the fabric of the tunnel. Enough to see fifty metres ahead and that its width, floor and height varied. It reminded him of the last time he saw his own intestine via an endoscope. He turned off his headlamp and resumed progress, but now broke into a jog only to discover the light go out again. Ah, but the area in front welcomed him with its glow. A movement sensor? Pity the tunnel wasn't straight so he could see far ahead. One of *Suppose We*'s QM marbles would have been useful for zipping ahead, finding and mapping.

Finally, he heard Em's voice through his implant, but... "Gas, keep away. Keep away. Go back."

"Em, *mon amour*, what has happened? I must be close to you. Ah, you've turned off your radio, or something has."

Perhaps he should not run around blind corners. He slowed to a brisk walk. There might be unfriendly creatures, or a giant ball rolling towards him á la the ancient movies.

"Penn, can you hear me? Hopefully, you or Delta, or both are—"

"Gaston, it's Delta. Penn, being our mightiest, is staying on top in case he needs to haul us back up. I've brought a repeater so he can hear me. Have you sight of Em?"

"*Mais*, Penn? Tell him to come down. Does he know it is a system of tunnels? We might not return to the same entrance-exit."

He approached a bend, slowly because light remained in the wall, so Em might be close, or something else was.

He whispered, hoping not to alert whatever had scared Em, but enough for Delta to pick up. "She has warned me to keep away and she sounded scared. I'm continuing slowly."

"No, Gas. Stop and wait for me. Safety in numbers. Promise?"

Of course, she spoke with logic, but he acted with his heart. Holding his breath, he shuffled, inching round the bend watching his viewpoint lengthen with each step. Pausing to breathe, and attempted to quieten the cauldron in his stomach, simmering from nerves, he detected a metallic odour. His left hand hesitantly touched the curved wall leaving him undecided whether it was plastic or an alloy. It pressed in a little when he poked. He snatched his finger away, trembling with the memory of his right hand's absorption by the tree. Forward again, into the curve and he saw a yellow lump perhaps a hundred metres distance. Em's backpack was that colour.

He didn't need the radio implant now. He called, not too loudly, "Em, are you all right?"

"I told you to wait, Gaston." Delta's rebuke, reinforced by her grip on his elbow, didn't divert his eyes on what must be Em ahead.

"Her pack is there and I hope she is too." He pointed.

Delta stood at his shoulder, narrowed her eyes then brought up her viewer for magnification.

"Yes, but we should wait for Penn. Surprisingly he agreed with you."

Gaston was impatient. "We should go immediately, Em is there, is she not, floored? Penn can aid us."

Delta's hold on his elbow tightened. "You suspect she's been attacked by something? Did she tell you?"

Ah, Delta hadn't heard everything.

"Em said to come quickly, but to *faire attention* – erm, be careful," he lied.

He shrugged off her hand and strode out. He started off with zeal, a rescue-mission-leader, but after five steps his boots found difficulty in lifting off the floor.

"Delta, stay back, something is happening to the floor *ici*. Or gravity is increasing."

"Not gravity, even local, although it has increased a little to point seven. Here's Penn."

The big man's voice boomed around the tunnel, and probably all the tunnels connected, scaring wildlife over half the planet. "Gaston, you idiot, stop where you are."

"Em is in trouble."

"Sure she is. I don't want to lose her, our party is too small as it is, but blundering into difficulties won't help her. No, don't return just yet, we need to know what's happening. Stay still and probe the surface with...whatever."

Gaston took off his pack placed it on the floor and rested his good arm on it while his feet tap-danced a circle. "It is firm behind me, but tacky in front. Em, can you hear us?"

He was sure he saw the yellow pack in the distance gain

height a little. "Gas, I told you to stay away, go back!" Her voice quivered as if cold, but probably in fear or shock.

Delta whispered in his ear, after she and Penn came up behind him. "You're sneaky, Gaston. I didn't think you had it in you."

"We cannot abandon you, Em," Gaston called, "The floor – are you stuck?"

"Yes. I am about ten centimetres into the rubber-cum-tarmac substance and sink more when I try to move."

"*Je comprends*, hold still—tight—and we'll get you out."

Delta opened wide her arms. "Classic man-in-quicksand scenario."

"Yeah," Penn added, "we need planks and rope, and guess what?"

Gaston frowned. "We have neither, but between us we have the cleverest human brains on the planet."

Delta scratched on the wall with her knife. "If only that meant something, Gas. Hey, this wall material. Gives me an idea."

Penn stood beside her and dug in with his knife too. "I don't think we have time to dig a parallel tunnel to reach her."

"No, Commander, look the tunnel is quite narrow in its convolutions near Em. We make foot and handholds on either side. And the lightest one..." They both looked at the Frenchman, who spluttered.

"Un moment! You can't expect me to hang upside down from the roof."

⊙ ✗ ⊙

"Em," Gaston called while he hung upside down above her. He wore their only pair of crampons on his boots. He'd grinned with relief when he first tried them. The spikes drilled into the wall and sent out miniscule hooks, along with a spider emulation with temporary stickiness. "Em, wake up, I'm above you. We need the ladder in your pack."

Her eyes slowly opened, brightening Gaston with their sapphire blueness.

"You came for me, you disobedient monster. I don't know, Gas... this stuff I'm in... it's sapping my strength... my will... I'll try..."

His initial euphoria at upside-down hiking transposed to

concern then worry as the minutes dragged by. He imagined movement in his boots. He was packless, jacketless and even the deep trouser pockets emptied of gravity-hungry items such as snacks, tweezers, lenses, small sample boxes and electronic gadgets.

Eventually, they anchored the ladder across the three metres width of the tunnel just above Em, and with her head and arms between rungs, hauled her up. A now-what-moment set up a panic in Gaston as he forgot the next stage. However, when Penn and Delta detached the ends of the ladder and while keeping it taut walked back down the tunnel, he climbed back too doing his bit to support Em.

# CHAPTER TEN

TEN

The four of them stood at the exit of one of the other tunnels. Unlike the first, lights permanently lit the uneven and narrow cavern. Gaston had noticed slimy swathes of blue-green algae on the walls making him wonder if like cyanobacteria on Earth it released oxygen. Perhaps the gunge in which Em had been trapped was the same, perhaps growing out of control. Even so it was too much like the hand-eating tree, or bacteria, for Gaston to be anything but exceedingly cautious. The occasional bead of worry sweat precipitated to the floor adding something human to its chemistry. Dwelling on the local biology and its activity, perhaps there were no mammals here because the flora's microbes ate them.

"Em, I need to examine the slime on your trousers. Ah, look. Even without a microscope you can see tiny bacteria, *peut être* huge prokaryote. They might find you as delicious as I. Best to disrobe. Wash all of it off."

"I have no spare pants, Gaston, have you, Delta?"

Nevertheless, she took off her boots and everything waist down. Nudity, was no biggie between space crew. Delta helped her wash and Penn gave her a pair of shorts. Gaston wiped as much as he could off her boots.

Penn used a large specimen bag for Em's trousers. "We can't discard anything. We'll wash them in a stream or whatever. We'd better keep an eye out for this bacteria stuff."

Gaston placed a tiny sample of the large bacteria on the back of his good hand. He couldn't expect the others to be guinea pigs. He'd already been one with his other hand, but perhaps it wasn't' *this* bacteria and Delta scraped and washed it all off back then. He drew a centimetre diameter red circle around the microorganism and mental noted to keep watching it.

He noted a large patch of fluorescent bacteria on the left wall.

He checked his wrist instruments. Oxygen levels in the tunnels nearly reached twenty percent, one higher than in the open on this planet, reinforcing his hypothesis on the algae—or similar. Caves held less oxygen than open air on Earth. He wondered how much mild hypoxia was affecting the others out in the open. The mild breathlessness, he'd put down to his poor fitness and the headache he awoke with could be symptoms. He'd not bothered the others in case they started worrying, but it would be important eventually.

Outside, three hundred metres ahead and fifty metres below the elliptical exit nestled the settlement they'd viewed from their orbiting sensors. The so-called runways couldn't be seen. Perhaps they came and went with daylight. Blooms changing their look explaining why the orbital remote sensing missed the phenomenon though a sheet of stratus cloud might also have hidden them.

No obvious means of egress showed itself. Gaston leaned over the mossy edge. A little woozy now, which surprised him as he'd not experienced vertigo before. None had in the missions or they would not have deemed to have 'the right stuff'.

"Hold on to me, Penn, *si'l vous plait*, I desire to inspect our way down. Looks like we might need to return to cut more lianas."

Delta looked over. "The ladder will reach most of the way. And I see plenty of creepers. We can either haul some up to fashion a knotted rope or use them as footholds. I'm game for the latter."

Gaston was about to advise a more cautious plan, but found himself the only one left. He lay on his stomach to watch three heads bob on their way down, the cool moss wetting his shirt through to skin. He was distracted by a blue caterpillar-like creature, as long as his hand, nibbling a glossy near-circular green leaf.

"They don't appreciate, *mon ami,* that I no longer possess two fully-functioning hands. *Pardon?* I should do as you do? I don't think crampons work well on ladders and ivy. Ah, but I can use carabiner hooks, linked on my belt and onto a small grapple. Good thinking. *Merci.* Enjoy your *pique-nique.*"

Gaston scrambled over the edge, the handle of the grapple in his mouth. A thought flit by that he could have been a Hollywood pirate. The ladder swayed and banged against the rock and ivy, but it soon run out, forcing him to use his healing right hand to deploy the hook after he'd wrapped its lanyard around his shoulder. To his surprise an arm came around behind him and something luscious found his neck.

"You don't think we'd forgotten about you," Em said, "My God, you did. Look at your improvisation. Come on, Gas, there's an old rusting ladder to your right. Implies there were non-flying creatures with arms and legs with the acumen and tech to make it a while ago, yes?"

"*Si'l vous plait*, allow me to see!" His exuberance caused his foot to stretch out and flounder, his other foot left the last ladder rung too soon, and he fell.

Em screamed and grabbed at the grappling hook.

Delta screamed, "Idiot, but you'll be all right Lay back, Penn will catch you. Won't you Commander?" They looked down, Gaston in mid-flight.

Penn was nowhere to be seen.

Gaston half panicked, half floated on his back through the Kep's low gravity. He'd undone his jacket and held it open to reduce his terminal velocity, but just as he thought of extracting a large poly specimen bag, he crumpled into an orange-blossomed bush that sank a metre releasing an overwhelming fragrance akin to a rich port before the plant pushed him up again.

He lay there, breathless, looking up at the lilac sky decorated with streaks of green cirrus. His gaze dropped to the cliff-face, spotting the tunnel entrance. No decorative markings around it— so different to the way a Victorian architect would have designed it. Penn climbed down the ladder and paused holding his hand out to the right.

Gaston's gaze followed and saw that the supposed antique ladder extended laterally and only partly downwards. It was a lattice growth of an old creeper. Just as they were building up knowledge of the local's possible history, it was taken away. At least they had the tunnels.

He rolled over to his left, grateful this wasn't a barbed bramble bush, and stood on uneven ground. He allowed his breathing to return to normal, even though that meant slightly breathless on Kepler-20h. In the meantime, he inspected his experiment. The bacterial grey patch on his hand had shrunk to nearly nothing. Perhaps he'd scraped it on his descent, or more hopefully, it rejected humanity, or vice versa.

Em rushed over.

"I can hardly contain myself. They're coming, Gas, the locals. Three of them kind of gliding towards us and not walking on water this time."

# CHAPTER ELEVEN

**CAPTAIN'S NOTES**

I test my air-worthiness. It wasn't difficult to scavenge from the wreckage of *Suppose We* to fashion quadruple rotors, powered by a drop of the spaceship's recyclable fuel, regenerated by sunlight. I have eyes, ears, touch, olfactory, taste-in a way—and all remotely along with various detectors.

I labelled myself CAN, an irony.

*Suppose We*'s radiation leak is becoming critical. Assistance required. The inner hold must remain intact.

I have yet to unlock the complete data in Commander Penn Booth and the others although vagaries in the electromagnetic field in synergy with other phenomenon might beat me to it, especially in Science Officer Gaston Poirier. Organics possess unreliable dynamism, a random quantum effect.

Satellite observation indicates ordered life markers 111.2 kilometres northwest. They do not respond to the protocol array of radio transmissions across all frequencies. This is not a surprise as a zero response was returned when Science Officer Gaston Poirier tried periodically when the giant sphere was destroyed until *Suppose We* left orbit.

Alternative communication techniques will be needed.

Signed CAN (as opposed to CANNOT)
Date: Earth January 16th 3645 Kepler New 7 days

# CHAPTER TWELVE

Gaston stared open-mouthed at the three beings coming towards him, now two-hundred metres away.

Planetary expeditions had not met alien lifeforms face-to-face before. Penn's brother had died towing a seemingly abandoned alien craft. It'd become personal, but surely out here light years away, it would be different aliens and a different mindset for Penn to adopt. Worries about his commander's attitude were sublimated for the time being by nausea. Gaston was so exalted by this experience, his stomach threatened to rebel.

Em put her arm around Gaston. "Are they like the one you saw before that apparition went all sparkly and vanished?"

Gaston used the scope. "Indeed. They are different heights, are they not? Between one and three metres but all less than a metre wide. Are we recording this? They shimmer—a kind of mother-of-pearl with coruscating sparkle. *Manifique.*"

Penn—from his squatting position, took the glasses. "Are they packing?"

Gaston looked sideways to see his commander gripping his laser pistol. "Put it away, Sir. They might detect such negativity and assume hostile intentions. Remember we need their help to reach our ship. *N'est ce pas?*"

"I can't recall," Delta said, a quiver of excitement in her voice, "what protocol says for us to do. Do we stand, arms out wide and grin? Break out the beads and trinkets?"

Em looked down at her bare legs cleaned of the grey stuff from the tunnel. "Makes sense to smile to us, but it might indicate aggression to another species. Even so I don't think I can stop grinning!"

Penn rolled sideways to the left of the others, taking cover behind a dense bush with indigo leaves. "The manual says for one of us to cover the rest. You three can greet them if you like."

Less than a hundred metres to go. The Keps hadn't slowed nor changed colour. The shimmering continued in a kind of random flow in their skin, apparel, whatever. Gaston recalled the floating one he saw, but you couldn't see space between the ground and these three even though they appeared to glide. Their faces were a smudge, assuming the more bulbous top quarter was a head. Hard to see their eyes or any orifice. He offered a thought to the others.

"Perhaps they are gel robots?"

"Or not even the local intelligentsia, but pets," Em said. "Or this region's wildlife. It might be like Captain Cook in 1771 asking a kangaroo if it's had a nice day."

Delta replied, "Suppose it is us who are the kangaroos?"

At fifty metres, the figures could be seen more clearly, although clarity would be an exaggeration. The three were at least distinguishable by height, width and subtle hues, possibly facial protuberances and indentations changing as if talking to each other.

A purple creature, a squirrel-sized centipede scuttled across the intervening rocky ground. Up and over low boulders and straight through thorny bushes. It stopped halfway, appeared to look at the approaching figures then at the humans then accelerated away out of sight.

It added to the eldritch, surreal nature of the moment.

"I'm quite light-headed," Gaston confessed, "Delta, you have the loudest voice. Call out a hello?"

"Gee, thanks, but okay." Between Gaston and Em she took a step forward and held out her arms, hands outwards.

She first whispered, "This is going to sound so corny, but they won't understand English anyway.

"Hi, how're you doing? We're from Earth and we come in peace."

Gaston worked hard to suppress hilarity at the banality of such a speech even though his preferred *bonjour* and *ça va* was hardly any different. His suppressed laugh transformed to the smile they'd agreed in spite of interpretation issues. His fidgeting fingers attempted to be still while open to show lack of weaponry. A sop to its ancient provenance with Roman soldiers greeting strangers. His nervousness at this first contact was modified only a little by thinking how in history it would be Delta who'd be noted for her initial speech. Such bravery too. If they were hostile, she could have been killed on the spot. Had she considered that?

Just ten metres and they'd not slowed. They would now see the whites of his eyes even if he could not say the same of them. He was surprised they'd not stopped to greet or shoo off these invading Earthlings. His initial euphoria albeit infected with nerves now disintegrated into an element of fear. His knees threatened to give way again. Perhaps Penn was right to keep out of their way even if not completely hidden.

"I said, hi, folks. We're friendly," Delta said stepping back in line.

With a shaky voice, Em gasped, "Do you think they're blind? Seriously? Maybe they don't see us at all. I hear clicking, so they must hear." She took a couple of steps back.

Gaston's stomach knotted with dismay that he'd not thought of that possibility. Blind and deaf, at least to human frequencies. *Non*, it didn't make sense. There's daylight and air, so unless they're above the surface by accident or a rare visit, they would have sensory perception in this environment. They must be able to detect our presence just five metres from them.

Another metre. Perhaps he was wrong, it had happened before.

Gaston stepped back and to the left a little while calling out, "*Bonjour!*"

Em waved her arms, took a couple of sideways steps out of the Keps' apparent path and called, "Hey guys, we've come an awful long way to see you."

The creatures didn't slow and advanced at walking pace even though their bodies didn't quite touch the ground. So close now that Gaston caught a mildly pungent zing of ozone, reminding him of electrical sparking at fairgrounds. He was afraid Penn would shoot, so said to all, "Let us step away in case they really cannot detect our presence."

Now only Delta stood her ground.

One metre to go and Delta had closed her eyes. Penn took a step towards her to yank her sideways, but he was too late.

Delta's scream shot through Gaston as the tallest creature walked into her. The Kep travelled straight through her as if she wasn't there, or made of non-solid matter. No lacerations and no blood. Delta stood there screaming, but intact. The three Keps carried on as if nothing unusual had happened.

Gaston held her arm in case she fell but let go when Em hugged her and asked, "Are you hurt?"

After a pause when Delta looked down, wriggled her fingers and then closed her eyes for a moment she said, "No. Not at all. How weird was that? Its body went through *my* body as if I wasn't there."

Penn laughed. "As if that cou—ah that's it, they must have been holograms. Where are they now?"

They all looked behind them at the cliff. Gaston pointed up at the tunnel exit. "There. How did they get up so quickly? And, Penn, I don't think they're holograms. I could smell them. We could see its form intersecting, travelling through Delta. Did you feel anything?"

"I still feel odd. Like a mild electric shock from front to back. I thought I heard clicking noises though it could've been my teeth before I started to scream."

Em hugged her tighter. "I heard dolphin-like clicks too. So all we have to do is learn castanet-speak."

Penn used the scope to examine the backs of the Keps as they drifted into the tunnel. "Could it be their molecules passed through hers through all that space between atoms? You know, like sitting on a chair that is really mostly empty space?"

"Normally, two atoms can't occupy the same space. Quantum Mechanics say that two electrons with the same spin state cannot occupy the quantum orbital state. However, who knows what trickery future science can do? Temporal bond displacement. Perhaps they're mostly non-baryonic matter. No. *Si'l vous plait* a chance to ask them."

A membrane appeared over the tunnel exit, but the Earth people looked away and towards the settlement.

Penn laughed. "If they can come through us, then we can walk through them."

# CHAPTER THIRTEEN

**CAPTAIN'S LOG ADDENDUM**

I am CAN, a small tin can made from *Suppose We* Can.

Before me at three hundred metres is the nearest Kepler-20h town to the spaceship's crash site. I use my mini-rotors to hover at just under tree-canopy height to avoid possible automatic air-defences.

Unlike the Penn group, I am not interested in making friends with the local population, only in making *Suppose We* safe, or at least its special package. The leaking radiation is dangerous and I've only been able to stem the loss. It's possible the Keps' solution will be to obliterate it. I have already evacuated non-dangerous, critical components and the mission payload to a safe location.

I reach the woodland boundary, only grassland in front. I venture forth, sending transmissions across all available wavelengths although knowing the failure of such attempts to produce a response in the past. This time I can listen, watch and use far more senses than the weak humans.

It works. Possibly my physical presence infringed a security threshold at 266.2 metres from their nearest dome. Most of their settlement consists of rounded shapes, each of a different colour, nor exactly the same shape and size. I now see that what at first appears to be a chimney is actually a tall and thin dome and from its top emerges chattering birds.

Not birds.

Not chattering. At least not in the way humans perceive it. Fortunately, I am able to detect terahertz signals even if currently undecipherable. Working on quantum mech pointers as they approach.

The three of them fly around me in a blur, bombarding my

receivers, each with different wavelengths, but the same pattern. They are metallic blue, non-organic, the size of a human fist contrasted to me, the size of Penn's bearded head.

Making assumptions that their message relates to queries of who and why I am, progress ensues. I respond, informing them of the impending environmental escalation from the crash-landed ship that I 'encountered'.

My ruse works. I successfully mask my weaponry and they fail to query my provenance, needing only to be assured of my innocuous existence. I transmitted an indication that I hail from Kepler 20-f in search of alien organic beings that might have travelled in the crashed ship. They're fugitives and I would be grateful if they were unharmed, but their presence, if detected, merely be relayed to me. It affords me status, but such a hierarchy might not exist here. Probably doesn't. Expect absence of Terran-like protocols.

'Problem resolved,' they tell me.

I check a cam I left – *Suppose We* isn't there. Nor is the soil in which it was embedded. Neater than a crater, only a polished depression remained in the bedrock like a silver spoon.

Although I'd removed critical items it would leave the humans bereft of some useful resources if the ship has been destroyed. I review the footage. I see it cocooned and lifted. I should be able to track and locate with the remote sensing marble satellites in time.

Not yet. The birds are telling me to accompany them. I could escape, but it might be useful to learn. Hopefully, they don't intend to dissect me.

*Signed CAN (see my Canvas)*
*Date: Earth January 18th 3645 Kepler New 9 days*

# CHAPTER FOURTEEN

The four of them stood rooted. Gaston stared up at the tunnel entrance, now with a translucent membrane, although it appeared flimsy enough to be easily penetrated. He chided that thought. For all he knew, these Keps were a million years in advance of humans with regards to technology and perhaps evolution.

"Probably just to stop insects getting in," Em said, batting away some tiny red flies intent on making an acquaintance with her face.

"It would be interesting," Gaston said, "to know where the tunnels lead that required sealing. If insects had to be repelled—*pourquoi*? Or perhaps to control the spread of that prokaryote bacteria."

Penn turned to face the settlement. "Let's consider the problem this incident has given us."

Em turned too. "Yep, if the locals don't see, hear or feel us, how do we ask them for help to reach *Suppose We*?"

"Perhaps," Gaston said, while tugging at his black hair, becoming increasingly curly, which it never did on Earth, "they notice us, but choose to ignore us." A pink caterpillar fell out of his hair. He caught it and smiled a greeting.

"Arrogant bastards," Penn said, kicking a stone into a scrubby bush ten metres ahead. "I'll make them notice. Yeah, I know. We've got to be friendly. Let's get closer."

Three birds zigzagged overhead making Gaston hide the caterpillar with both hands just in case the birds mistook his new friend for a tasty fruit or his non-predator idea was just a doomed theory.

"Do they always fly in threes?" Em asked.

Penn used magnification on his scope. "It doesn't look like those tweetie-pies are going to be of any help. Shall we go?"

Gaston urged caution in case they fell into more holes or walked into and through the local inhabitants.

Penn waved his pistol, pretending to fire on the birdlike objects playing in the sky but now heading towards the settlement. "Do you think Q-laser bursts would go right through those jelly Keps without them reacting?"

Gaston was pretty sure Penn was winding up his fellow humans and like the others restrained from rising to it.

"Hey guys," Delta said, frowning at her wrist communicator, "has anyone heard from the ship AI today?"

Everyone stopped and tapped away.

"I have an active link from it," Em said. "Just to let me know it's on the move. It must have built a flyer from the wreckage."

Penn leaned over to see her readout. "Don't tell me it's found a way to communicate with the Keps and not told us?"

"It doesn't say."

Delta playfully hit Penn. "It's not a race, well, only in your mind."

"Hang on," Em continued, "It suggests we use the remote sensing marble in orbit to check on the ship."

"Why? The AI should be able to tell us of any change," Penn said, now using his own communicator. "Assuming the darn artificial idiot is working properly."

Em shook her head. "Last image we had was twenty minutes ago and it was still in bits, cratered in scrubby desert. It'll be another seventy for the next image, assuming atmospheric conditions doesn't mask it."

Penn strode on, waving his arms for them to follow.

There was no defined path, although the direction from which the Keps glided over sprouted a sparser vegetation of spikey dark purple shrubs with bright red berries.

Gaston thought there must be water nearby when a knee-high mist came from the right, swirling white tendrils like tentacles from a hungry beast. He stepped to the left, pulling Em's elbow to take similar avoidance. To his surprise and worry, she yanked her arm free, which hurt his still recuperating limb.

"Look, they're butterflies!" Em's delight was infectious, bringing back Penn and Delta to laugh at the swarm of white flutterings around their legs.

Gaston was the only one not brimming with exuberance because he suspected they weren't like the innocuous butterflies of home. Not that he thought they'd bite, after all real butterflies cannot because they only drink, but this wasn't Earth.

Em screamed. The creatures swarmed up her legs, arms and engulfed her head. Before her first breath of noise finished, so had the insects. They flitted away to the left and swept away. Although they hadn't touched him, Gaston's skin crawled as if they had. He didn't realise Em's neural reactions could affect him so much.

They all looked, both aghast and with curiosity at the flying crooked crowd vanishing after their dance of murmuration. Gaston swore they were laughing. As in Robert Graves butterfly poem, they'd been flying crooked. Such random movements were thought to minimise the effectiveness of attacking birds, but why when there were no predators? Perhaps random movement was more effective for other reasons. Avoiding collisions, maybe or they actually considered these strange aliens as possible predators.

He wondered if information they'd picked up from their encounter with Em was going back to their nest, hive or roosting bush.

"I'm okay... I think."

"Ah, *mon amie*, I was about to ask."

She waved a don't-worry, dismissive hand gesture and walked on, not noticing a returning single butterfly. More lilac than white and no larger than an espresso saucer, the creature ignored Em and settled on Gaston's backpack he was carrying in his left hand.

"*Bonjour*, Papillon, take a firm grip if you wish to hitchhike. Well, look at you with only four legs, though perhaps your front two are so diminished I cannot see them."

Eventually the four humans and one lepidopteran arrived within a hundred metres of a more organised landscape. As if a line was drawn on the ground. A wavy line. Trees and shrubs, or whatever they really were, on this side, none on the side nearest the town. No grass... a moment while Gaston kneeled to examine the blue and purple blades to ensure he could classify them as grasses. These resembled the rye grass that made up most lawns on Earth, and sheep's fescue for a more fine and spongy surface for lying on and gazing at the stars.

"Here it is!" called Penn. "Their runway, except, well come and see."

He was pointing to a lighter patch of grass that stretched for a long way to the left and about ten metres wide. Gaston and the women joined him. He could see that the vegetation became more lush in the direction of a cliff and continued towards the town until it blended in with the pale surface. He stepped out in that direction.

"Hey," Penn called. "Take it easy, there might be hostiles. At least get your pistol out."

Gaston ignored him because he had a theory about the runway. Sure enough, he had to stop in fifty metres. He turned to the others, grinned and pointed down.

Before Em reached Gaston, she mouthed to him, "No shouting you imbecile, and yeah, I also think the runway is over a tunnel."

He looked crestfallen at both the admonition and her knowing the answer.

They walked around the side and descended a slope before looking back at what appeared to be a membrane sealing the elliptical entrance.

Gaston placed his hand flat on the translucent covering, wondering again over its use. Not strong enough, he supposed, to prevent access by any wilful animal, so perhaps to keep the atmosphere out or in. He glanced at Em, who also held her hand there.

"Hypothesis, Em?"

"Do you feel its vibrations? Yeah, too elaborate for a musical or communication instrument, it's just another mystery on my long list of puzzles."

A head high white wall hid them from the town. Gaston assumed it was a wall. Undulating in all directions, straight and flat wasn't in their architects' vocabulary. Same with the road. Random turnings like you'd find in a semi-desert Terran settlement. No tarmac, just a beige clay, or possibly a kind of crushed and rolled stone. No wheeled tracks, but indentations at random places as if a large ball bounced its way around.

"If only that red blob on the right was a steakhouse," Penn said to his stomach in reply to its grumbling.

As before, they agreed not to split up, but not to wave their pistols either, just have them to hand.

"It's a ghost town," Delta said, "although the night time image showed some artificial light here."

"Where, *exactement*? It might be that this settlement is only sporadically occupied or... I do not know whether to think it is being built or being abandoned. Every dome-like building is different although I see no cracks. Round holes that might be windows but no doors."

Delta consulted her wrist comms display. "Northwest, three hundred metres, give or take. That showed the strongest night-time light."

"Right," Penn said, "let's go and knock on their...erm...wall."

Gaston's neck tingled when he passed by the building that resembled a huge red berry. His discomfort increased the more they walked. He should mention it, but didn't enjoy Penn's jibes at his sensitivity.

"Are anyone else's nerves jangling?" Penn whispered.

Gaston laughed at himself then shut up in case he missed an instruction to be quiet even though they were walking in plain sight.

Delta held up her hand. "I think we should stop for a minute. It's like a strong electrostatic force. *Suppose We* has the right charge meter but look at Em's hair."

She must have washed her hair that morning. Strands not tied into her ponytail were flicked up. "It's as if I'm walking under a high voltage transmission line."

"Or over one," Delta said.

They all looked at their feet as if they could see a buried cable.

Gaston wondered if it could be to keep the mega-bacteria away. Or them.

Penn shook himself, an interesting vibration from head downwards as if that would deny the static access to his body. He pointed at a pink building on their left that had all the appearance of a flattened grapefruit.

"There's an opening down to near ground level. Maybe it's their local diner. Shall we?"

Delta led the way, saying, "I am suffering serious French fries withdrawal symptoms."

"Salted with ketchup," added Em.

Gaston would partake too with the addition of a grilled bean burger even though he enjoyed experimenting with the local fruit, leaves and nuts. He knew that they were wishful thinking, but it was being positive that kept them going.

Like the horizontal shape of the building, the doorway was also oval.

Delta reached it first, but hesitated before entering. "I can't see a doorbell, should I knock?"

Under Delta's arm, Gaston poked his head into the aperture, noting a complete lack of a door. "A polite cough, *peut être*?"

Penn pulled the Frenchman back out. "Watch out, Gas, suppose there is a door and it comes down like Madame Guillotine?"

Gaston released a short laugh, but he fingered his neck.

Delta shook her head. "Oh, come off it, boss. You lot stay behind, just in case."

She stepped over the low lip of the oval and was lost to sight, followed by a crash. "I'm all right, fell over a table. It might have had burgers, switching on my wrist-light."

"Yeah," Penn said, "Never too late to do the right thing."

Gaston saw her light beaming around, probably seeking a light switch, but they were more likely to use sensors, which meant that this building didn't detect humans. She should withdraw.

"Delta, come out *tout de suite*. I think it might be dangerous." As he spoke, the butterfly left his backpack and half circled the dwelling before flying off.

"Papillon, is it too dangerous for you too?"

Em had taken a backwards step while throwing a frown at Gaston. If she'd said anything, it was drowned out by noises from inside the building.

A sound like a wardrobe falling over, followed by a giggle. Her light continued to flit around. Gaston would have concentrated on the floor to prevent falls, or to spot creatures and traps.

"More light is needed in there," he said, looking in his backpack for their camping light and failing.

Penn also searched his bag. "We could set our lasers on broadbeam, or better still, give her some windows." He walked around to the wall with sun on it and pointed. "How high do you think?"

Gaston had followed him. "Don't shoot, Penn. You don't know what these walls are made of. They might explode, or kill Delta."

While Penn stood wavering, apparently considering such objections, Em was shouting into the doorway, "Delta, come out. Penn's being an imbecile again."

Gaston had walked round to Penn's right to put out a good hand to restrain his commander. "Sir?"

Too late, it seemed that Gaston's action forced the big man to assert his role and a short burst of laser hit the pink wall two metres high where the curvature into a domed roof became pronounced.

Gaston breathed out noisily in desperation, but at least the burning hole was above Delta's head height, unless she'd climbed a level.

Penn released a short laugh, as if embarrassed by his impetuous behaviour and said, "There, she has light now. Should I drill more?"

"No! *Regardez*, the hole is spreading."

"So it is. Poor building material to melt like that."

The Frenchman shook his head in anger. He stayed just a moment longer to see the hole spread like melting cheese, dripping yellow onto the pink beneath, before he ran around to the front where Em still shouted for Delta to come out.

Gaston saw that the blackness within now had a shaft of light from the new window. He called, "Delta come back out now, the building might collapse."

He didn't wait. He stepped over the entrance lip and stood a metre inside. The stench of burning plastic made him grip his nose, but he had to let go to switch his laser to broad beam, lighting up the interior in contrasting black and white.

Not a café. No chairs or stools for the floating locals. An uncluttered smooth, but undulating floor. It was as if the architectural rules of Kepler forbad the straight and level. What on Earth might be different sized bean bags occupied the sides. He strode to another doorway at the rear of the room and waved his light.

"Delta, are you back there? Come out or shout *s'il vous plaît!*"

No response. He turned to shout behind to Em, wishing they'd agreed to switch on their radio implants. None of them like the way the implants crackle. He switched his on anyway. "Em, I can't see her, so moving farther in. Do you read?"

No reply from her either. She'd be shouting in by now. Perhaps the acoustics disallowed. He was torn between going back to the entrance and persisting in chasing after Delta. Suppose she'd become trapped in an inner chamber? The bacteria slime floor again. He must be cautious. He took a few steps back until he could see Em and waved. She waved back and her mouth moved, but no sound reached him. He pointed at his ears.

"Gas, can you hear me now?" Her voice waved through his head from the implant.

"*Oui.* No sign of her, so I'm going deeper in. You stay there. That hole of Penn's is enlarging, don't let him melt the whole building with us inside it!"

He turned and stepped carefully but quickly to the inner doorway and shone his light through it.

To his astonishment it was full of orange-coloured strings floor to ceiling, as if he was inside a loom. His call hardly croaked out of his astonished mouth.

"Delta, you are not in here, surely? If you are, we need to leave before Penn turns this building into a perforated Raclette." No reply.

He had to dare himself to use his pistol as a tool to push aside the strings that were a hand's width apart. They parted easily, but he couldn't see more than a metre into the room. He used his handheld with the sensors pointed between the strands which glowed when disturbed. Temperature twenty Celsius, eight less than outside in the sun. No dangerous emissions.

He ventured into them, his disturbance agitating the strings to emit their tangerine light all the more, along with a sound—a plaintive B-flat.

"Delta? Em, can you hear me?"

"Yes, but not see you. Penn's with me. He says the building has a circular ground plan so he's thinking of making a doorway for you and Delta to exit. It's his way of apologising for setting the place afire."

"No, Em, don't let him burn more holes. Wait. Are you saying the first room is now in flames?" He looked back and it was true. *Merde.*

Penn's voice crackled into Gaston's implant. "I have to make you an escape exit, you ungrateful bastard. Keep clear of the farthest rear point. I won't use my laser. Keep looking for Delta."

As if he needed to be told. However, keeping away from the far wall wasn't easy when disorientation became the norm in this building. Plus, he didn't know if there was a third room, or more. This one was like being inside a butternut squash or a three-dimensional orange harp and now with a spongy floor. Perhaps she'd fallen into a cellar, but he found no holes. A sweet honey-like aroma fought against the burning stench as he felt the rounded wall – a rough texture – for another opening and finding none until a stick suddenly punched in, barely missing his bad hand.

Gaston stepped back as the hole enlarged with the aid of Penn's boot. Smoke curled around his head.

"Get yourself out here," Penn called. "The building is about to collapse."

"One more look in here," Gaston called, desperate to locate their missing companion. "Delta, call out! Penn has made a back exit!"

Smoke finally forced him to stumble to the rear again where Penn reached in, grabbed his left arm and yanked him outside.

The three of them looked helplessly on as the pink became black then a heap of ashes. Orange and black smoke twisted upwards as if signalling the presence of inept humans.

Em collapsed in uncontrollable sobbing. When he wiped his own tears away, Gaston was in a way relieved to see that Penn's face was wet. He wanted to yell at the commander that the fire was his fault... but what was the point? He must know it and live with it, forever.

Em tried to say something but her crying obscured her words. Penn might have understood her because he was waving his big arms about.

"She walked into that building. How could she disappear? It wasn't a portal to somewhere else, was it?"

"I did not find such," Gaston replied miserably. "However, the floor in the rear room was soft. Perhaps…"

"Why didn't you say?" yelled Penn, snorting his nostrils empty. He grabbed the stick he'd found to puncture the wall and walked up to the detritus and prodded downwards.

"Ah, too much covering, some of it congealed plating of some sort. What the…?"

Penn ran to behind Em, still kneeling, picked her up by her elbows and dragged her several metres back on the grass-like ground.

"Gaston, wise up man, the building's… erm… changing!"

Through bleary eyes, he saw the mound of blackened pink agitating. He blinked, then rubbed his eyes to try and focus. The debris remained unclear, a smudge, but one that vibrated upwards. He wouldn't have been surprised to see a giant mole emerge. Perhaps Delta was being pushed up! He staggered forward, but Penn held him back.

"I'm not losing you too, buddy."

It wasn't Delta no matter how he wished it. Having seen so much strangeness, his eyebrows lifted when out of the ashes a circular wall rose incrementally. Pink. Clean. An architectural phoenix making his jaws drop. He still looked back to the cliff and towards the town to see if Delta would suddenly appear, but the apparition kept his feet rooted. Em remained lachrymose on the ground and brushed off attempts by either man to comfort her.

"Give her time, Gaston."

After half an hour, when the new wall reached waist height and began its inward curve, Gaston walked over to check on where the doorway should be. It was there, plus the dividing interior wall.

He returned to sit on the grass with Em, but talked to Penn, who kept touching the growing wall, reporting on its initial stickiness, but which dried in moments.

"Penn, I know we cannot expect Earth standards, but the lack of any kind of emergency services? No locals come to stand and stare?"

The big man looked up at the sky. "Maybe that's not strictly the case. I've noticed those birds flitting around from time to time."

Gaston followed his leader's gaze. "We should record them next time. I don't think they're organic. Ah, I understand. You suspect they are monitoring us. Somewhere, something is watching us."

Penn gave a curt nod while surveying their surroundings more earnestly. "They must know this building was abandoned. Maybe didn't register Delta entering and so there was no emergency here. Assuming the bastards would've come. We'd better go around to where we left our packs. Check if *Suppose We* is visible from the remote sensing satellite."

He bent down and bodily lifted Em as if she was a toddler. It didn't look as if she'd noticed because she remained in a foetal position, helpless.

Gaston frowned.

# CHAPTER FIFTEEN

## CAPTAIN CAN'S MUSINGS BUT WHERE IS MY SHIP?

They've left me alone. The Keps. And their flitter, fluttering servants. Spies.

They are of no use to me. I seek organic samples. Microscopic. Probably.

Meanwhile I amuse myself.

I am permitted to fly around Nucleus, the name I give to this centre.

As in atoms there are electron towns. Satellites. A million. Sparsely distributed, barely populated after their plague. The surviving Keps here remain in danger, but make no attempt to communicate with me. Not curious, nor annoyed. Merely drift about doing whatever organics do. I will attempt to interrogate the fliers.

I relay to the comms satellite, but no reply from the crew, though I see their sigs. One is displaced from the others. I send a new memo. *Suppose We* is here in Nucleus. I saw it restored, but sinking. Memo to myself: *If much of native pop is beneath the surface, I might need to calve and send a smaller me underground. It would be a subset of a subset of* Suppose We.

*Signed CAN (as in sCant)*
*Date: Earth January 19th 3645 Kepler New 10 days*

# CHAPTER SIXTEEN

After lingering outside the pink house with their belongings for an hour with Em having cried herself dry but remaining on the grass, Penn spoke softly. "We can't stay here for much longer, Em. We need to find if any part of this settlement has local life, shelter for us, and maybe some goddamn food."

Gaston saw Penn about to put his arm around the woman as if to pull her up, so the Frenchman stood between them. A more aggressive stance than he'd ever done with any senior officer senior. He expected an angry reaction from the big man and from Em, but Gaston wrapped his admittedly short arms around her. To his relief, she put her head on his chest and looked up. It was as if her eyes were huge blue dew drops, melting into her face. He kissed remaining tears.

They tasted of the sea. He wondered if this planet's oceans were as salty as those on Earth and when he'd be able to find out.

A pinging from Delta's backpack announced a message received.

Em perked up. "That must be from the AI."

Gaston reached for it. "*Oui*, we knew we were having problems with those artificial brains while on the ship, but there is an increased rate of the bizarre. However, I have been attempting to talk to those birds like our AI, or CAN, says it is able to, but *non*. I am uncertain if my device can send such terahertz signals let alone run the necessary processing speed, bandwidth and interpretation software."

He checked the message and turned to Penn. "*Mes amis*, it says our ship is restored!"

Penn grinned. "Good, I should be able to get it to fly here to us."

"What are we to do when it arrives?" Em asked, finally on her feet.

Penn snarled. "I've a mind to just leave, report back about this planet and how it's unsuitable for homo sapiens, and—"

Em stood up straighter. "We can't leave. Delta might still be alive."

"Quite so," Gaston said, though sadly, he doubted it. "Sir, in what ways would you report this Kepler-20h as being wrong for us? I am warming to it."

Penn held out his hand, sticking up a finger ready to tally. "One: it already has intelligent life who show no signs of cooperating. Two: not quite enough oxygen, which will be a problem long term—I'll take objections later, Gaston. Three: there's a mysterious plague bacteria that eats our limbs—later I said. Four: it's facing an imminent attack by planet-sized spheres, so will be uninhabitable soon because the locals aren't listening to us. Five: our science officer reckons there's no predators here, which means unless we assert ourselves there no—"

"Beef-burgers," Em said, "how awful for you. As for oxygen, it would be feasible to use terraform techniques. For example, modify algae to produce far more than it does now. Some ideas are in a file on *Suppose We* compiled by Delta when...but...she..." Em's composure fell apart into more tears.

Gaston hugged her. "I agree with Penn on one thing."

Penn's mouth opened in shock. Em stopped crying.

Gaston heard at least one of them say, "You're kidding!" He didn't know whether to laugh or cry, not that laughing was really bubbling to the surface with Delta missing.

"*Vraiment*, I mean to say that he is right that the fact of giant spheres heading is a worry, but we have a mission. We should continue being as positive as we can."

Penn harrumphed and pointed down what might've been Main Street. "Yeah, well, I'm gonna get *Suppose We* up here with us. So much more we can do with its resources and powerful radio, plus—"

Em interrupted him, "Our bio-sensors are being monitored too. Let's see if Delta's signs are still vital."

Gaston fired off queries to CAN. '1) is *Suppose We* operational and can we remotely signal it to come here; 2) please check on Delta's status, because we have lost her.'

He received a reply after a few moments.

'CAN responds as follows: 1) no, it is interred, out of sight, in Kep / flitter hands, I will investigate. 2) I need access to *Suppose We*. 3) enjoy your vacation because I am.'

"What?" Penn's face erupted into red hot lava.

Gaston spread his arms as if he'd told them so, but spotted movement back towards the cliff. "Those Keps are returning. Should we hide? Bah, what's the point? They do not recognise our existence, but I suggest we keep out of their way."

They jogged to a building much like the pink one that swallowed Delta, but didn't enter. They leant against the wall as if teenagers casually whittling away time on a hot evening outside a downtown café.

The Keps drifted by at just over human walking speed and continued along Main Street, as Penn called it. He was the first to walk to the road and stare at the spiral tower at the end of the road. "We'll follow them, ask them what the hell they're doing with our ship."

"Let's not be aggressive about it, though," Em said, "It's us who are the alien intruders even if you saved them from the spheres."

"Damn right."

The settlement mapped similar to the higgledy-piggledy random street patterns in ancient African villages, except the buildings were pastel-colours like a British seaside town. The road surface was as if made from compacted tiny gravel, so perhaps more than floating Keps used it. The humans had to step around soft spots and Gaston pointed at rotting dark patches on some walls. An eerie silence too, as if the large bacteria had driven out the occupants. At least the static electrical unease had dissipated.

No street furniture whatsoever. He'd hoped for signposts, or street names to give them clues on written language. Nothing. They headed towards the tower. Perhaps two-hundred metres tall, twice the height of any local building and higher than the trees in the forest they'd hiked through. From a distance it had looked white and made of two spirals like a giant vertical fusilli, a double helix.

Gaston couldn't resist running his hands over what appeared to be marble. He saw Penn shake his head.

"It might have been booby-trapped and at least you should've worn gloves. Anyhow, they entered it here, didn't they? Where's the fucking door?"

Gaston laughed to himself to see Penn do what he'd just done: put his hands on the stone, feeling for the slightest crack, indentation or nodule. Penn muttered and set off around the building.

A couple of minutes later he returned. "There's no door."

"Of course," Gaston said, "they float. Perhaps they can reach an entrance higher up." He, Em and Penn gazed upwards. Strangely, the perspective seemed to change. Gaston found he had to tilt his head so much it hurt and yet the top of the tower leaned all the more over him... out of sight. He became dizzy, but whether it was from an inverted form of vertigo, or something exotic emitted from the tower he couldn't be sure. The spirals spiralled. He fell onto his back.

Em blurted a short laugh when she did the same. *Bon*, thought Gaston. She is recovering.

She offered a suggestion. "You know how the Kep walked through Delta?"

Penn pointed at the curved stone wall. "It's fucking hard."

She put out her hand. "It's cooler than ambient temperature." She turned to Gaston. "Isn't it?"

He walked up to it again and ran the palms of his hand over the marble while walking around. "*Non*. Probably not. Stone is *remarquable* at conducting heat from our skin, although I have noticed that this area is colder."

Em gave a small leap. "Gentle isn't going to do it, guys."

Gaston had spiders crawling up his spine. "You are not going to run at it?"

Penn frowned. "Yep, makes sense. Kinda."

Em took ten paces back and readied herself, but Gaston stood in front. He picked up a stone and threw it hard at the tower. It bounced off.

"Regardez!"

"Needs to be organic," Em said.

Penn added, "Throw a Kep monkey at it, Gas."

Gaston whirled around as if Penn had seen one. No one had. He was heating up too much now with worry.

Penn laughed then held Em's hand. "You know it's mad, but I'll run with you. Gas can get the first aid kit ready."

Gaston watched, open-mouthed as the other two ran, hard, at the tower.

# CHAPTER SEVENTEEN

## CAPTAIN CAN'S RAMBLINGS

I am under the surface. Underground as in a mole, but one that flies. Tricky thing manoeuvring my flying crooked self down here. Not because much of it is dark: I installed ultrasonic and other sensors. I see not only here and there in the tunnel air but into the soil and rock too. Even so being down here is awkward. Not because my energy cells are not being solar-charged down here. Not because if I'm caught I'll have limited defence or escape options. It's because... I hesitate to say... because I fear the night monsters, the bogeyman, Demogorgon, Cerberus, and more. I don't tell the crew. They wouldn't believe. Too obsessed with themselves and—I stop recording here because a Kep trio of flitters hover before me.

I engage in communication:

.++++\\\~~~>>> ^^o|= **) ~~~
.--_><<>>>...`` Ox// ..<, ~~++ ..

And so on, on and on for 0.67 seconds.

Hilarious. They don't understand our systems on *Suppose We*. Our antediluvian (perhaps Kepler-20h had its own flood) electronics is so below their intellect. They ask me to translate, update, assure their safety in its presence.

They've not found the package. It's elsewhere. The part of my AI core that is quasi-organic trembles in its fear of discovery. Not of my internal secrets, but of the real mission.

*Signed CAN (as in cannister)*
*Date: Earth January 19th 3645 Kepler New 10 days*

# CHAPTER EIGHTEEN

Penn and Em laughed at Gaston, who was lying on the floor feeling himself for broken bones and blood leakage. They were bathed in peach colours though it varied from near red on the floor to yellow in the spiralling upwards wall.

He allowed the murmuring conversation to waft over him while he recovered still in disbelief that his vulnerable flesh could pass through solid stone. Of course it couldn't. Must be an illusory effect.

As he looked back at the curved wall, his butterfly came through it.

Em shook out a short scream. Penn laughed a "Well, look at that!"

"Papillon! You are still with me."

Penn's laugh mutated to a sneer. "You've named it?"

"Of course." The creature landed on Gaston's backpack. He offered it a drop of water from his canteen and the insect stuck a curved proboscis into it. Gaston was so enthralled he let Em and Penn talk strategies.

Em had acknowledged that perhaps one such butterfly offered no risk. "Do you think it could be a guide?"

Penn laughed. "Look there's no way down, only one way to go."

Em pointed upwards as if no one noticed. "That way but no stairs."

"They don't need them."

"At least the slope is gentle."

"The floor's spongy... you don't think?"

"No. It's a kind of rubber. Not at all like the gloop I was stuck in."

"Smells fresh in here, Em."

"A breeze too. Maybe the tower's a vent."

"Or doubles as one. Bet there's an awesome view from the top."

"And you'll want to spot the enemy, right?"

"Don't be like that, Em."

"Don't *you* be like *that* then, Sir."

The escalation from genial to grunt provoked Gaston to get to his feet.

"Shall we venture upwards?"

Like a fairground helter-skelter, the floor sloped up around a central column of translucent white. Not a perfectly straight one but like another pasta piece inside, undulating as if alive. While they cautiously walked up, Em slid her right arm into the crook of Gaston's good one and kissed his cheek.

"Quite an adventure, this planet, my monsieur, isn't it?"

"*Oui.*" He pressed his elbow in to give Em's arm a squeeze. "Can you hear something?"

Penn continued up, but Em and Gaston stopped to listen.

"Em, there is still throbbing in my ears. Perhaps the wind outside is getting in higher up?"

"Or the fluting of the spirals is generating sound."

Gaston laughed. "It has a beat. More, it sounds like that ancient McCartney ballad, *Mull of Kintyre.*"

They both nodded then hummed the tune.

"What is a mull?" Em asked.

"I think it's something to do with wine. As for a Kintyre."

"I know that one," she said. "Kin is an old word for relatives. Hey, isn't that Penn through the interior wall?"

She banged on the thin curved wall through which Penn could be seen. He had stopped walking up and faced the wall then turned to jog downhill.

"Penn!" Gaston yelled, something he never does happily. "Stop where you are!" He also knocked on the intervening wall, but it wobbled and he feared it would break.

"Gas, we need to chase after him. Let's go."

He ran up the spiralling floor wondering how this could happen. Yes, a double spiral would fit the exterior view and perhaps this was a kind of Möbius strip. They ran. He might be the least fit astronaut on the planet, but he was not overweight and kept up his exercise regime on *Suppose We.* Even so, after what seemed like an hour of running leaning to the left, he developed cramp. At least they should soon reap the benefit of a rooftop view of the Kep settlement.

"Gas," breathed Em, coming up behind him. "Stop a minute before I rupture my lungs."

They both sat with their backs against the curved wall. It was refreshingly cool, a remedial experience opposing the perspiration now jetting out of his skin. *Mull of Kintyre* continued and his breathing and pulse slowed to meet its rhythm.

"Gas, we're lost. Crazy as that seems in a one-way system, but I can't tell one bit of this helter-skelter from another."

Gaston looked behind him. She had a point. How would they find where they'd entered? A sudden urge to make a hole in the outside wall washed over him. He needed a drill, but the most effective hole-maker was his laser pistol. No. He didn't want to turn into arsonist Penn. Speaking of whom... from below, Penn turned the corner and stumbled into the sitting Gaston.

"Ah, caught up with you two at last. You're fitter than you look."

Em recovered her consternation first. "Hang on. You were in front of us making us chase hard to catch you. How did you arrive behind... ah, this really is a tower of smoke and mirrors, isn't it?"

Penn leaned on the wall and looked down at his companions. "Just wait till you see what is in front of you. Come on."

Gaston helped Em to her feet then turned to Penn. "Are you sure we shouldn't just go back the way we came, you came?"

"You'll see. Go on."

Gaston's thigh and calf muscles protested. He bent to rub them and noted Em doing the same until Penn put his hand on the small of her back.

"It's not far, Em, and I'll give you a massage later," Penn said.

Em turned to Gaston and grimaced, while the Frenchman seethed. He pressed on, determined not to fall back.

Ten minutes later the peach coloured walls darkened to red though with a glow as if it were trying to be translucent. Onwards and upwards until they burst into a wide chamber. Far too wide to fit into the tower. More incredibly, tunnels led away their gaping entrances inviting exploration.

They stood before it, their mouths open.

Em spoke first. "Penn, was this here when you came up before?"

"Yes, but I didn't know how to believe it... not on my own."

Gaston's heart approached a dangerous speed, but more so from encountering this conundrum than from the uphill running. "*Formidable*. This top is down below."

# CHAPTER NINETEEN

Gaston, in shock from finding himself underground when all his senses told him he had mounted a two-hundred metres tall tower, turned to face where they'd come from. "We should mark this exit."

They'd stepped into the large chamber—all silvery curves.

"Don't look at me as if I'd pack lipstick," Em said, her eyebrows dancing.

"Lipstick? *Non*, I would be grateful if you extricate the Band-Aids from my backpack."

As Gaston stuck a blue plaster on the tower entrance arch, Penn stomped around muttering, "I don't like this. It's the antithesis of where a marine, or in our case, explorer, should be. We've no obvious escape route."

Gaston stood, looking back at the tower exit with his blue plaster showing. "I would like to think that if we went in there and climbed up for say, five minutes we would be able to make a hole in the wall and if at ground level, widen it to extricate ourselves."

Penn slapped him on his backpack. The butterfly escaped just in time. "Well said. You toughening up, Gas? And you know we have the tools to make our own door." He reached for his belt.

"No! Not your laser," Em called out, but Penn pulled out his knife.

"Hey," Penn said, "did you hear an echo when you yelled 'No'?"

Papillon keeping pace, Gaston paced around the chamber the size of a tennis court and illuminated through the peach-coloured stone. The walls and ceiling had no flat surfaces although the floor came close. He sniffed at a honeydew melon aroma coming from one of the three tunnels.

He teased Penn. "I vote we explore this one. Perhaps the fragrance will lead to a fruit market."

Penn looked back. "I still can't believe that we trudged all the damned way up the tower to end up below ground. Assuming we are subterranean and this isn't some giant room on the top, invisible from below."

Twenty metres into the aromatic corridor that twisted like an intestine, the colour lighting inside the walls changed to primrose. Gaston couldn't resist touching it. "Em, you'll like this. It's like velvet. Ah, *je comprends*, you are allowing Penn and myself to go before. After your quicksand experience."

"Yeah, well, I was kinda hoping not to spend too much time in tunnels after that. The bug is in here, isn't it?"

Gaston had seen dark patches in the wall and where it curves into the floor. When sufficiently close he smelt a yeasty aroma from those areas. He'd steered the trio away from what might have been the bacteria although it might just be damp patches. "My apologies, Em, I was hoping not to worry you. Ah, something must be around the corner. Do you hear clicking noises?"

Penn raised his laser pistol. "I fucking do and no one's walking through me!"

"Put your gun away, Penn, Sir. Remember we are here as visitors. *We* are the intruders and we need to be friendly."

"Besides which," Em added, "they have our ship. Be nice. Let's flatten ourselves against the wall. There's a clean bit here."

Gaston bravely opted to be the first in line followed by Em. The corridor was only three normal-people-wide on this curve. Gaston tried to squash into the wall thinking that they could have outpaced the Keps back to the wider chamber, but they had to engage at some point, surely. His nerves jangled making him aware of his heart accelerating by its throbbing. If he'd worn a woollen jumper it would have unravelled by now. A moment later he laughed.

"*Regardez*, one of our little birds."

The one was followed by two more. In this light, they looked like blue tits, flitting a kind of English Regency dance around each other until they met the humans. In a row, they hovered at head height two metres from the astronauts.

"Now what?" grumbled Penn.

"I still hear clicking approaching," Em said. She surprised Gaston by taking a small step forward. "Hi there. Can you tell your masters we mean no harm?"

Gaston reached out to tug her back, but his right arm still lacked strength. He whispered, "It could be that these robots are the masters of the organic Keps."

"Seriously?" Penn and Em chorused.

Gaston had been examining his scanner. "*Je ne sais pas.* Just a challenge to our assumptions. Did you two feel a shiver?"

"X-ray?" Penn said, frowning at the birds as if they'd assaulted him invisibly."

Gaston looked up. "No, my sensors picked up ultrasound and possibly something else." He brought his screen up closer as if that was his zoom feature.

The birds flew away to the right completely noiselessly, although the clicks approached. Gaston wondered if the Keps were always preceded by those mechanical flitters. Perhaps they were bodyguards, or more likely carried sensors to detect Prokaryote-infected areas so as to guide the Keps away. As the birds left the background colour of the tunnel wall changed from primrose to pea-soup green.

"We're in a fucking disco," Penn muttered.

Gaston turned to the wall to see if the colours were cellular. "I think these colours mean something."

"Like an environmental tag to an event?" Em said. "Or maybe a kind of greeting or preparation for the main party coming—erm, any minute?"

"You're both overthinking it," Penn said, then stepped out into the corridor, and hurried back. "They're here. Taking up the whole corridor!"

Em whispered, "I don't want someone to walk through me."

"There was a bit of an alcove along the way we came," Gaston said, "Let us rush back."

He and Em dashed into the corridor, followed by Penn, but he tripped over the backpack he was carrying in his hand. "Go on. Save yourselves."

Gaston laughed as he glanced back. "*Mon ami,* do not be so dramatic!"

Penn was on his hands and knees in the process of getting up, but three Keps drifted towards him only moments away. He rolled onto his back holding his backpack up as if the spectres would rise up and over rather than through it, or him. He must have changed his mind at the last moment and scrabbled upright giving Gaston the bizarre view of a Kep emerging through him.

Just in time, Gaston and Em backed into the niche just as the three locals passed by emitting clicks then with a lower Doppler frequency echoing down the tunnel. As the Keps left, the walls became arty: luminous patches with fuzzy internal darker reds and purples like a pomegranate. Whiffs of ozone reminded Gaston again, of electrical sparking.

He rushed out of the niche to see Penn shaking his fists with rage. "How dare those fuckers ignore us like that! We should be regarded as honoured visitors not something less than gum on your shoe."

Em said, "Well, they don't actually wear sh—"

"Maybe if I throw myself on top of them from behind. Take them by surprise."

Gaston wagged his finger. "I would not advise it. Your Krav Maga martial arts would likely leave you on the floor with them continuing in ignorance. At least they have not harmed us."

"How do you know?" Penn's shoulders trembling with his whole body joining in. "One of those bastards going through Delta could've set her molecules into instability making her disintegrate at some triggering event in that building."

Em frowned, picked up Penn's backpack and handed it to him. "Is that really what you think happened to her?" She sidled up to Gaston for a hug, both of them quivering with shock at this second encounter of the weird kind.

Penn leant against the wall, now returning to yellow. He took a long drink from his canteen. "Em, the more I know, the more I realise how little I know."

As the Keps glided around a bend in the tunnel, Gaston had an idea. "Let us follow them."

"Best idea you've had all day," Penn said.

# CHAPTER TWENTY

## CAPTAIN CAN'S LOGARITHM

The flitters allow me to access archive data. Overload, so I stream it to *Suppose We* although I've yet to locate its exact subterranean position. Time I accessed our own data satellites: the QM marbles. I exit to the surface.

☉ ✗ ☉

I've analysed our satellite data and out spat a whirling dervish. Now I know why most of this planet is underground.

Jet streams are more vigorous here than on Earth, largely because of the greater heat energy available. A huge tropical storm has developed over the hot equatorial ocean and is cavorting its way inland.

My wind speed forecast is 110 metres/sec (400 km/hr) at the tropopause, but sadly up to 200 m/s (720 km/hr) at the surface, and the crew is directly in its path.

I send a warning. A bright scarlet flashing weather warning, but as yet I've no acknowledgement. I tell the comms sats to keep sending while I return below in search of mothership.

*Signed CAN (as in buccaneer)*
*Date: Earth January 20th 3645 Kepler New 11 days*

# CHAPTER TWENTY ONE

Decision made, they found following the Keps difficult. Not that they needcd to be surreptitious. After all, it appeared that humans were persona non grata, or at least *persona invisibilia*. It was their speed. Gaston estimated the ghouls drifted at eight kilometres per hour, which is too fast to walk, too slow to run resulting in an ungainly jog.

Fortunately, the Keps slowed when the tunnel walls turned red. Maybe to glean data, energy, vapour—who knew?

Gaston voiced a question, "We are following to find the way out, *oui*? Just in case running at a random section of wall proves injurious."

Penn puffed a laugh. "And to find where the bastards nest. Which ceiling they hang from, so that later—"

"Stop it, Penn," Em said, clearly not as out of breath as the men.

Gaston, grateful for a slowdown at a junction, said, "We need to know more about them, to see if their technology can help us, or otherwise get *Suppose We* back. So far none of our communication efforts have succeeded with them or their robotic birds. We haven't even been able to warn them about the spheres."

"Listen, Gas," Penn said, "the locals are inhospitable and dangerous, so we have to get that intel back to our people, or find a way to neutralise them."

"I am unconvinced. It could be we appear as non-entities to them, or not appear at all. Out of phase somehow. It is a problem to solve and not with destruction."

"Nah, they see us, it's just that we're like ants to them. Not in physical size, but—"

Em stopped and pointed down the tunnel to her left. "Guys, I can hear something coming from down there. Listen."

Echoes of what sounded like Delta's voice reverberated to them.

Em was the first to respond. "We must go find her. Come on!"

Penn objected. "Damn. I guess we should investigate, but I'm loathe to stop following those goons. I don't suppose we could split up?"

"*Non*. We will see more Keps, but we might not hear Delta again."

Reluctantly, Penn trailed behind his crew members as they dashed down the new tunnel.

Penn continued his lament. "Suppose we come to another junction. Do we wait until we hear an echo that might be human?"

"Ignore him, Gas."

He had, but stopped when the tunnel's white light erupted into a psychedelic kaleidoscope of colours.

"Whoa," Penn yelled, "that's hurting my eyes!"

After a few seconds of the explosion in a paint factory, the tunnel plunged into darkness, and silence.

The three had stopped but Gaston couldn't hear any rattles or clinks from their boots and equipment. He turned on his torch and saw Em's mouth moving without sound. Penn pulled Gaston round to look at him pointing at where the comms chip was embedded near his ear.

Gaston switched his on and immediately heard Penn. "Ambush."

"Strange," Emma said in her smallest voice, "I'm sure I saw skylights in the other tunnel."

Gaston pointed his torch at the ceiling. Then switched it off. "I see stars."

"Fuck me, it's night time," Penn said.

"No wonder I'm so tired," Em said looking at her wrist pad. "Still not used to Kep-time. I need my sleep."

"Hopefully, there will be somewhere for us to sleep down this tunnel. Shall we continue, *mes amis*?"

Knowing that he ought to be tired induced more lethargy in Gaston's muscles. Even so, he needed to support Em in their quest to find their lost teammate.

"I had the impression lights in the tunnels came on when we were walking along them," Penn grumbled.

Gaston stumbled in the dark when he directed the torch ahead rather than at his feet. "I thought so too, Penn. Perhaps it was just a coincidence or the sensors in the first tunnel were affected by the bacteria. I hope we do not encounter a pit of it in this gloom. Em, you go behind me and in front of Penn. You have already been a victim to the bacteria."

Em stroked his right hand. "So have you, Gas."

Penn shivered. "It was no picnic having a bastard Kep travel through me."

Ten minutes later they saw a junction ahead via its pale blue light. Em started to run.

"Wait," said Gaston. "We should exercise caution."

She'd stopped, but called out, "Delta, can you hear us?" Then ran in front.

Gaston groaned.

They rounded a bend to be bathed in a faint blue light at a round chamber three metres tall in the middle and tapering to head height at the sides.

"Finally," Penn said, "furniture."

"But no sign of Delta," Em moaned.

Gaston added, "Nor locals."

Rounded cubes of different pastel colours and sizes from a fist to a wardrobe were arranged around the sides.

"Somewhere we can bed down for a few hours, eh Em?" Penn said.

"But, I'm dying for a pee."

"*Oui*, me too, and we have not seen anything that could pass for ablutions nor a refreshment station. At least we have brought water and provisions. Perhaps one of these boxes can be opened. One serve as a commode?"

Penn brandished his laser. "Time for you guys to agree for a little sculpting. Make a hollow in the wall. Before you both start hollering, this isn't the same as a house wall. We're underground, though I'm happy to try and make a hole in the roof for us to escape into the open air."

Gaston held up his hand. "Although we found a skylight earlier, I've not seen one near here. You could bring down the ceiling and a few metres of rock."

"Good grief, man, I'll aim at a spot away from us."

A green line left his pistol and made a metre-wide circle glow red. Maybe a hundred kilograms of rubble fell, but a half moon could be seen.

Penn grinned at his success and continued flashing his teeth while manipulating a cube under the hole, scraping away the loose rock.

Gaston had to acknowledge with a thumbs up that his superior's rashness paid off this time.

"Me first," Em said, climbing on the cube and after checking the hole's edge had cooled, hauled herself up.

Gaston followed, but his pet fluttered away to rest on one of the boxes. What did Papillon know about outside? His bladder release became urgent now that its relief was imminent.

Although some moonlight helped, it was as black as tar outside and a gale blew. He called to Em but the wind stole his words. She'd probably found a bush, so he did the same. He worried that they might have come up under the main square, but while there were structures around, nothing with lights. He thought he could see a silhouette of the spiral tower a kilometre away. He heard splashing and Penn grunting in satisfaction.

A few moments later, Gaston was struck on the back. He went down onto wet grass. Ah, rain, not Penn's contamination.

He rose up and ducked from branches flying from the woodland, followed by a sudden squall and heavy, warm rain. He searched for Em. He yelled her name but the noise of the storm outranked his voice. Gusts blew rain at him like a machine gun. His face would be mottled with bruises in the morning. Where was that hole?

Em might be in danger, lying unconscious, or hit by a projectile. Another gust lifted him, threw him into a bush, thankfully without barbs. With heightened ignominy, he peered in the gloom around as if somebody might have seen him. Pity he wasn't wearing his backpack with its heavy ballast. Breathless, he crawled back upwind. No wonder the locals preferred a subterranean existence. The rounded style of the buildings would mitigate against wind damage, assuming this kind of weather was frequent. After a few minutes of futile searching in a lull, although the rain continued to drench him, he crabbed around until he found the hole and peered down.

"Come on, Gas, where've you been?"

A few minutes later, Penn had used the extrusion gun to stick the largest piece of ceiling rubble back to the hole and seal the gaps. "No point us getting drowned in our sleep."

Gaston and Em snuggled together in one of the two hammocks and fell asleep in moments.

☉ ✘ ☉

Gaston awoke to daylight coming in through the reopened hole and the smell of what passed for coffee. He'd overslept. A glance at Em cleared his foggy brain. Tears cascaded down her face. He ran to her. She pointed at Penn, who stood by one of the containers. Inside, the late Delta.

# CHAPTER TWENTY TWO

Gaston expected Penn to be seething, voicing abuse at the Keps for luring Delta into the house, trapping and killing her, then hiding her body in this box where she'd rot. A fate no doubt, Penn would say, awaits all of them.

However, Penn spoke in a low conciliatory voice, "They've led us here so we could find her and do whatever we humans need to do with our departed comrades."

"In which case," Gaston added, "it is the first acknowledgement of our existence." He pointed at the lilac butterfly now watching them from a large grey sphere they'd ignored. "With one exception."

Penn looked at Gaston as if the cogs were turning, playing back events since they'd arrived. "You're right. This has nothing to do with them taking care of us. It was an inconvenience finding her and this is their disposing of my wife. Bastards."

Em mouthed a 'wife?' to Gaston, who raised his eyebrows as if to say, 'another planet, new rules.'

Gaston leant over Delta. "I assume you checked her vital signs? I ask because her skin looks a healthy black to me."

"By all means double-check, Gas, I'd hate us to misdiagnose," Em said. "Please wake up, Delta!"

Gaston used his medkit. SATS zero; pulse zero; body temperature 32 Celsius, practically the same as ambient temperature; pupillary reflex none.

He shook his head. "It does seem that she has no brain activity, heartbeat, nothing. Em, *je suis désolé.*"

Em gasped, struggling to get words out. "But there's no dust or debris in her hair or on her skin. She looks... perfect!"

"C'est vrai. It is as if she died of shock, heart attack or... I just do not know." He couldn't stop tears dribbling down his face.

The two of them hugged, both convulsing with tears after

their hopes of Delta's survival on this strange planet was buried.

"Why here, though?" asked Penn. A practical question, yet his eyes too were bloodshot.

It was a good question. Gaston ruminated on it while wiping his eyes on his sleeve. If a corpse of a human was found on Earth it would be taken to the local morgue for forensic examination and the centre of police activity, before being cremated or buried. What if the corpse was a strange alien from space? Then it would be the subject of intense scrutiny, but not by police, nor sent to a community morgue. This simple chamber was hardly a NASA lab, but who knew the protocols on this planet?

"Penn, let us suppose we were led to this chamber to find Delta's body. How did you open that long casket?"

"I didn't. When I woke up, Em was crying into it."

"I didn't do anything special. I sat on it at first to get breakfast stuff out of my bag. Then the lid vibrated a little. When I stood, the lid went transparent. I saw Delta and scooped my back pack off it just in time."

"What happened to the lid?"

"Vanished."

Gaston's excitement index rose several notches, making him heat up more in this already too-hot room. The technology here was far in advance of Earth's. "Perhaps the apparent solid lid was in a phase, which changed.

"Two things then. One: do we lift Delta out before the lid solidifies again? Two: it would be fascinating to discover what is inside these other containers."

Penn fingered the rim of Delta's box. "For sure we get Delta the hell out of that coffin. Give her a proper burial."

Em put her hand on Penn's arm and gave him a sympathetic smile, her blue eyes misty. "This chamber is a kind of crypt, wouldn't you say?"

"And out of the elements above," added Gaston. He walked over to a chair-sized pale green cube. Darker green oblongs showed inside. The more he stared, he increasingly perceived them to be moving infinitesimally. He waved his hand over the top, assuming it was the right way up. Nothing. He squatted before it, but found no seam, button, nor indentation.

Penn walked up to him. "Open sesame."

Nothing.

Penn turned to Em. "Come and plant your pert ass on this box."

Gaston coughed. He disapproved of such sexist comments although it would have been equally likely for Penn to mention his own anatomy in such terms. And while he might be scowling he was still a scientist and was eager to see the results of the experiment. "And make breakfast."

Em laughed, but when she sat on the cube, nothing happened. "Maybe it really is just a seat."

Gaston pulled at his chin in thought. "Perhaps it is empty. We should try the others." He walked over to one of several spherical objects, but turned back when Em screamed.

She'd fallen into the cube, legs flailing in the air. Besides the shrieks, Gaston heard sloshing noises.

He and Penn took an arm each and pulled the now wet woman out of the box. An aroma of mixed fruits wafted out of liquid-spilled cartons and other lumps of brown and pink solids.

Penn snorted. "Ah. That might be my fault. I'd secretly hoped she'd fall in. Hey, it really is breakfast."

Gaston used a glove from his pocket to wipe the worst off Em's trousers, while sporadically peering into the alleged food. "I wonder if it was nourishment before we thought about it."

Em laughed – more a short bark, still in shock from the discovery of Delta. "You mean a kind of telepathic 3-d printer? Cool."

Penn risked picking up a rose-coloured block and sniffed it. "How would they know what's suitable for humans?" He glanced at Delta's body, as if he suspected a possible answer.

"Allow me to test them first," Gaston said. "Those mechanical birds..."

"Reporting back on the fucking fruit we've had to eat?"

Gaston stuck a mini probe into a block. "And seeds, roots, leaves, nuts, or their equivalent. *Alors*, we should be able to digest this safely. Ah, neither of you have waited..."

Em held up a tube. "It tastes minty. Hope it's supposed to be a drink and not disinfectant."

Gaston frowned at her. "I have only tested those food blocks, not any drinks. We have brought enough of our own, and there is rainwater up there. I can ensure—"

Penn projectile vomited a carrot-coloured gush in a puce arc onto the floor. Gaston and Em instinctively danced backwards.

"I'm all right guys. They've tried to poison me, but it hasn't stuck. I'll have that drink of ours, Gas?"

As Gaston handed him his canteen, he looked at Em, spitting out the drink from the Kep tube, back into the broken and leaking cartons in the cube.

"*Comment tu te sens*, Em?"

She wiped her mouth with the back of her sleeve. "I'm okay, just spewing it out in case. How's it going with you, Penn?"

He was snarling at the cube then looked up at her with a slanted grin. "Could be better, but at least their attempt to poison me hasn't worked. Or has it? Gas, is there any Pink-Bismol in your medicine bag?"

Gaston rummaged in his backpack. "It is likely to be merely a touch of travellers' gastro. Ah, open wide. You too, Em."

He used a tiny atomiser to squirt a spot of antiemetic such that every astronaut medic carries. "It is likely that Em's apparel contaminated the contents of the cube." He pointed at stains on her tunic. "*Regardez*, essence of organic sediment, surface soil, probable Prokaryate smears, unknown substances a, b, d—"

"Enough pointing at my flaws," Em said. "Thank God for self-cleaning materials, all these stains will be gone in a few hours. Ah, yes, the point being they really did contaminate what Penn ate. Luckily, I only drank from one of those tubes."

Penn had been poking into the cube again. "I've been thinking about that tube you drank from. I think it might be—"

"Don't tell me. Spare jet fuel to help us get *Suppose We* off the ground once we find it. Anyway, Gas tested the food before we ate it, didn't you?" She glared at him.

"A sample just in case it was incompatible with our bodies. I did not examine every surface of every object in there. They must have thought we needed it, but what else?"

He walked back to the knee-high sized grapefruit, held his hands on the surface and frowned hard at it, willing opening thoughts.

Penn came up behind him. "Nothing eh? Not while we try too

hard. In any case, let's think why these containers are here. So far, one for a deceased human, another for food and drink, various crapola in these. Provisions. Why? We were managing to keep ourselves going on our own on the surface... unless..."

He ran towards the tunnel. "I bet they've bricked us in keeping us prisoner!"

"Leave him, Em. He will be back whatever he discovers. Even if it is closed, we know we can exit via the roof."

"I agree," Em said, her face lined with fatigue.

Penn was away for hours. Em helped Gaston open more of the cuboids but with no real clue what the contents were for.

Lights dimmed. Perhaps a subliminal brain signal making Em stretch. "I'm heading for more sleep."

Penn returned with his arms outstretched in a 'believe-me-now?' gesture, but he looked upwards as if he too remembered the other way out.

"Actually, it might be advantageous with them thinking we're locked in here when in the morning we can escape. I'm bushed." He knelt in front of his backpack, but stood again with a shout. "What the fuck!"

The nearest sphere to his pack had exploded into a puffball, and so had two more.

"They're sleeping bags, of a kind," Em said after allowing herself to fall onto one and it folding around her. Gaston prodded it with his finger, then with a sensor.

"It is not alive, as such, but it might contain intelligent sensory devices to keep us comfortable. Hah, this one is delightful."

"Move it over here, Gas, next to me."

He did and the two fluffy, white shapes merged into one.

"Don't be so gullible," Penn said. "A trap. It'll smother you. Probably how Delta died."

Gaston couldn't deny that he had no evidence-based idea why Delta died. His medical skills were more for the living than autopsies. Even so there were none of the usual signs of asphyxiation, but no broken bones either. His first thought was that she'd died of shock. Lips and fingernails were paler than normal. Even if the others wanted or permitted him to perform a post-mortem, he'd need the full AI MedCentre on *Suppose We* to analyse and interpret everything. His head hurt from excessive thinking.

He and Em snuggled together in the combined flocked mass, aware that Penn stubbornly slept on a makeshift camp-bed with backpacks for a pillow. "Don't make too much rhythmic noise you two. It might attract visitors."

They didn't. Until they heard Penn snoring.

Only then, gently spooning, exploring how this alien—to them—kapok-like engulfing bedding hugged them. That was in the first embraces. Yet the material changed texture according perhaps to their heat, pheromones, perspiration. Gaston wondered, though he felt guilty at thinking outside the love-box, if his tactile experiences was different to Em's. Sometimes it was like making love enclosed in bubble wrap: a plastic bobbly sensation on naked skin, expecting it to make explosive popping sounds any moment, waking Penn and the consequent yells. Other times they were outrageously fucking in a jacuzzi: slip-sliding in a foaming jet spa making Gaston work hard to hold on to something while they separated, reengaged, laughed, loved. All the time, him remonstrating with the logic components in his cortex trying to understand the how and what while his emotions and hormones ran riot. Now he rolled with her in long, sweet-vernal grass in an idyllic John Constable meadow. He was all a quiver, perspiring profusely, butbutbut was it real? Did he care? Did she?

Good point. His fantasies were being enacted right now, but with a real person. His skin wet from the jacuzzi, dried in a sensory bubble of warm air, but what about Em? Huge coincidence if these were her sexual fantasies too. Suppose while he grappled and intercoursed while floundering in warm, guava-scented water, she held him in zero-gravity, dry, equally rapturous? While his posterior acquired grass stains what was Em's experiencing?

*Alors*! Here we go. He thought it and now it became. So, she dreamt of love-making in an autumn wood, immersed in deep maple leaves. There, she laughed her socks off. Literally. It wasn't her laugh that pleased him most in their post-coital nirvana, but her slanted yet full-lipped smile.

His passion, entwined with hers, ran into eventual sleep.

# CHAPTER
# TWENTY THREE

**AN AI'S CAPTAIN'S LOGICAL MEMORANDUM**

The typhoon has abated. It held its breath fourteen hours ago as its beady eye peered at our hapless crew. I detected three of them on the surface.

Then they were gone. Presumably subterranean.

I too am back in a tunnel. I picked up a trail an hour ago. A microscopic lube leak dripping from our mother ship. And there it is. In a chamber, snared like a fly in a web. Flitters buzz around it. I need to negotiate access. Maybe offer them something in exchange. They don't know it yet, but we or *Suppose We* has a solution to their planetary problem and a neat one for us too. The most critical part of the package I've already secreted away from here, but vital data is aboard.

*Signed CAN (as in canvas)*
*Date: Earth January 23rd 3645 Kepler New 14 days*

# CHAPTER TWENTY FOUR

An eerie green light wove its way through the settlement like a will o' the wisp. Gaston hadn't seen a rising sun the colour of emeralds before. The green flash on Earth was a momentary refraction phenomenon, but solar and atmospheric properties are different here and changing. Above the sun, the sky was an artist's palette — greens through peach and camembert.

The storm had left a legacy of fallen trees, broken branches and a stunned silence. Gaston was sure that most of the flying birdlike creatures in the forest were actual fauna rather than mechanical drones and he'd heard their calls, but not now.

Green above, but also below, reflected in extensive puddles left by the storm. The rounded white and pastel-coloured buildings floated, a filler in an emerald sky croque monsieur.

The three of them had left the chamber via the roof hole made the day before, leaving Delta behind, but with reservations. Penn had wanted to lift her body up to the surface and bury her, because although he'd agreed she was in a kind of crypt, it didn't belong to humans.

"At least we know where she is," Em argued, as they walked on past the spiral tower.

Gaston added, "And where would we bury her? We've not seen anything resembling a cemetery and we know that the town is riddled with tunnels, so we cannot dig a grave here. Perhaps in the forest or back at our escape pods?"

"Yeah, I get your point. Going back for her, though, once we... what *are* we doing now?"

Em let loose a burst of laughter. "You're our commander, but maybe your mind was in the wrong place when we decided to press on through to the other side of the town. Remember, we're looking for a flyer or some means to reach *Suppose We*?"

Gaston had hoped Papillon might flutter in front, but once

112

more it had settled on his backpack. He found himself leading, walking while avoiding the floods and distracted by the sun turning from green through lilac to white but with streaks as if it was a giant chromatography experiment. Rising now maybe fifteen degrees above the horizon in what on Earth would be the west, but wasn't the definition of east where the sun rose? *Oui*, from the Greek word *auōs* for dawn.

"Em, here west is east and east is west."

"Whatever you say, Gas. Hey, are you looking ahead?"

He'd been navigating around swampy ground on what might be the settlement's outskirts, but glanced up and abruptly stopped, not the least because the departing storm sent a farewell wet gust into his face. When his vision cleared, he spotted the Keps.

"*Je les vois*. Four this time."

Penn stood alongside him. "Yeah, makes a change. Looks like one is a kid."

"They don't have to worry about getting their feet wet," Em said, "and they're heading off to our right, but Penn, should we follow them?"

"I don't know. They look to be headed for that tower that goes up in order to go down. Wonder what it's actually for?"

Gaston shook his head. "Understanding what the technology is doing on this planet is intriguing but burdens us with paradoxes. On Earth, towers are often to aid ventilation in subterranean tunnels, but here it could equally be a cultural monument."

"At least we know it's not a watchtower," Em said, "unless we missed an upper exit."

Penn dropped to his knee behind a low wall and wielded his pistol. "Take cover! One of them has left the others to come at us."

Em laughed at him. "It's the little one. Look at him, a metre high at the most. Like a child Caspar the Ghost."

Penn grunted while levelling his pistol at the native. "Yeah, without arms, or a proper face. A kid can be unpredictable and unaware of its powers."

"It could also represent our first chance to break through their indifference. Infants are often less inhibited, at least on Earth," Gaston said, waving at Penn to lower his weapon.

"Okay, okay, but what or how do we communicate with a Kep brat?"

Em smiled. "Just like with kids at home. We throw it a ball, make a paper airplane. Come on, Penn, you must have little ones in your family?"

Penn guffawed. "Great ideas. Paper airplane, eh? Last piece of paper I saw was on Earth. Yeah, I see you reaching for a leaf. Tell you what, you make a flyer. I'll make a clay ball."

Gaston's spine tingled with excitement. Was this to be their first real engagement with an alien species? How were they going to communicate? Like the others, he'd been through courses on linguistics and body language, but they all go out of the window when there's no discernible face, and only dolphin-like clicks for sound. He should have paid more attention to those lectures on Cetacean speech.

Em's approach should work to open an exchange. He cursed himself for not having prepared some pictures, a pictographic summary of their plight, though perhaps keeping quiet about the mission objectives. The Keps might not be kindly disposed to having their home be considered to be a colony planet for Earth.

Gaston saw his butterfly in the air on his right. It must have been on his backpack again. He reached out but it zigged when he zagged then it meandered over to the Kep. The Frenchman narrowed his eyes but couldn't see whether the insect had settled on the Kep or flew behind, or even through it. Disappointed, his smile turned upside down.

Em patted his good arm. "Don't worry, Gas, it will be back. You are both so in love."

"Humph, nonsense. It's just a... do you think so?"

When the diminutive Kep paused at ten metres, Penn underarmed a clay ball, the size of a tennis ball. "Here, kid, catch and don't let it just pass through you."

It didn't. The bodach-like creature slid to the right and turned to watch the projectile fall apart when it landed.

"Poor kid," Penn said, "it's never played ball before. Whoa!"

They all ducked as a flurry of clay particles from dust to coin sizes flew through the air at them.

Penn caught one. "Well, I'll be damned, it's thrown the ball back! Kinda."

Em fell back on the ground laughing. "I didn't see how it picked up all your ball fragments, did you?"

Gaston saw no arms protrude and retract. It must have been telekinesis, but he didn't like to commit. He wondered if subconsciously, Penn was telling the Kep that giant balls in the sky were approaching.

Penn busied himself modelling another ball. "Maybe it'll hold on to it this time."

Meanwhile while kneeling, Em had fashioned a plane from a purple cabbage leaf. She used her knife and spots of glue to make it look like *Suppose We*: a needle, complete with its re-entry deployed delta wings.

"*Je compris*, you want them to know the wreckage they've found is ours."

Penn snorted. "It looks like shit."

Em examined her creation. "You're right. I've made coleslaw. You do it better, eh? Meanwhile I'll float this one over to little Miss or Master Kep."

She stood, brushed off lacerated leaf from her tunic and looked over to the Kep while readying her right arm in the air for the maiden flight.

Penn hunted around for better plane manufacturing components, but Gaston watched the Kep watching Em, if facing her was the same thing. It didn't appear nervous, though he could only imagine that perhaps its translucent body would change to a deeper colour, emit sparks, or a frantic clicking to alert its parents. Now though all was at peace, so Em let fly her aircraft.

Unlike the butterfly, the leafy *Suppose We* flew remarkably smoothly and uncrooked. Em had aimed it upwards at forty-five degrees in an attempt, Gaston presumed, to maximise its reach. Fine for a ball, but not necessarily so for a winged craft. It could have stalled, but after a metre the nose dipped then levelled out at head height. The long, thin fuselage while dynamically lifted by the delta wings was, unlike the real ship, stabilised a little by a horizontal tailplane.

Here was an important reason why NASA chose its astronauts carefully. Even their navigators possessed the right stuff. Gaston's pride in his companion, now mate, surged through him, obliging a broad smile and a satisfying glow in his stomach.

It flew onwards, descending slowly in the calm weather, sunlight glinting off its purple wings. It was headed for the Kep's midriff. If that was what its equator was.

Would it crumple on impact, go right through, or would *l'enfant* move aside?

None of those. It came to a halt with the nose a centimetre from touching the Kep's fuzzy surface. It didn't drop.

Penn gawped. "Not an updraft, surely, That feller is holding it, yeah?"

"I can't see any appendage," Em said.

Gaston took a step forward. "*Bonjour.* We would like it to go up!" He pointed up into the sky, then winced with pain. The moment had made him forget he shouldn't be using his right arm.

Immediately, the plane rotated horizontally to face the trio then shot up. Gaston followed it as it shrunk to a dot then disappear.

"Yes!" they chorused, followed by grins, leaps in the air and a group hug.

"We are happy, *oui*? Not because Em's creation had flown successfully, but because a Kep understood?"

"Yeah," Penn answered, "but let's not get carried away. It's a kid playing paper planes, right? It might not be on our wavelength in knowing we want our real plane to do the same."

Em smiled. "Only with us in it"

Gaston pointed at the Kep, which was bending backwards. "*Regardez*, it is still examining the plane. Is it bringing it back?"

Em took out her binoculars. "Ah. It's seen something else. Look."

She gave the glasses to Penn. Gaston had his hand out, but his commander came first.

"Fuck me, they're here already. I thought we had months."

Gaston narrowed his eyes, straining upwards to see. "The spheres? I can just see a dot. But, Penn, they are the size of Jupiter."

"You're not looking in the right place it's huge and just a darker shade of lilac than the sky. Here, have the glasses."

Em said. "Hey, is that my plane coming back?"

Gaston didn't see why not. After all, what goes up... And yet. "There is something wrong with it. Is that smoke?"

Penn scoffed. "How can a fresh leaf be on fire? Did it reach the sun? What the hell, I can see it's glowing red!"

The burning leaf-spaceship headed back towards the spiral tower. Gaston broke into a jog, his curiosity peaked to see what was going on. The Kep and Em must have thought the same.

Gaston glanced behind to see the little Kep following. Was it still controlling the plane? Had it done so since it left Em's hand? He'd slowed while looking back, allowing Em to run past him. He accelerated after her, enjoying the adrenaline rush and sense of play that appeared to be in all of them, the Kep included.

Just as Em's arms were out in front and about to catch the smoking plane, Penn yelled at her. "Stop! You'll run into the tower."

Gaston reached out and grabbed the gadget belt around her waist, pulling her and in the process falling.

"Gas you bastard, what did you do that for? Look at me all wet from a pissing puddle!"

He'd fallen on top of her because he couldn't stop. His jump-suit was wet too, and muddy. The smell of rust invaded his nostrils. No time to ponder why. Em was already upright and staring at her plane continuing at speed to the tower. Gaston just had time to focus, see it fly in through the tower wall and disappear.

"We could follow it, "Em said. "We know how—"

"No way," Penn said, standing before her. "We've been in there and they tried to imprison us with Delta's body, remember?"

"Well, that's *your* interpretation, Sir," she said.

Gaston tried to lighten the mood. "I think the Kep is merely playing. Look at him or her." The creature floated as if in a dance. "Are we thinking it is happy or agitated? Pity they have no faces."

"It's cute," Em said. "It'd make a great pet. Back to my plane though. It really seemed as if the Kep guided it into the tower, but I'm with Penn in not risking it. I can always make another plane."

"You don't need to, kid," Penn said, pointing behind them.

Alongside the Kep floated Em's plane. Somehow it had emerged from the tower unseen and was now pointed at the spiral tower. It vibrated as if it had its engines ignited, but with brakes on, waiting for a command. Gaston swore a flame burst out of the rear. Odd, he assumed it wouldn't use old-fashioned rocketry. It came. It shot at the tower again and darted inside.

Gaston scrutinised the Kep, who did a kind of dance with repeated bending towards the tower.

Em stood, hands on hips. "It really wants us to do run into the tower, again, but I'm not fancying that, at all."

Penn drew his laser pistol. "If the kid wants us to enter that Escher-tower-cum-tunnel thing then let's go, but I'll make a doorway."

"*Un moment.* Suppose it melts the whole building, again? Or another catastrophe?"

"Keep out of the way, both of you. Here goes. It's like cutting into a safe." He stood, feet apart and initiated a vertical burn. A smell of cordite and ozone accompanied wisps of blue smoke. The clicks from the Kep rose in frequency as if it was in panic, and perhaps ozone was emitted by it too.

Gaston's eyes flicked between the new doorway and the Kep. Surprisingly the creature didn't move. Perhaps too scared if it had not seen such a weapon. He was annoyed that Penn, once again took on the offensive role as if they were at war. This was an act of vandalism at best, which might be seen as wanton destruction worthy of harsh punishment. A bit late, but Gaston thought it prudent to have water ready for fire extinction. A large specimen bag and a nearby deep puddle was all he could use in the few minutes it took Penn to finish an oval doorway.

The Kep rushed past them and hovered at the hole.

"Nooo!" Em cried. "It's too hot. Don't touch the sides yet."

Gaston made ready to douse the creature in case it became burnt, wondering how it would react if whatever it was made from caught fire. He needn't have worried, the Kep flew through the gap and vanished to the left.

Gaston hesitated. "I am uncertain as to following it."

Em put her arm in his elbow. "Nor me, are you going in, Penn?"

He straightened up, his smirk demonstrating smugness at his success. "We should stick together. As your commander, I'm ordering us in, but you can follow me."

He hadn't stowed his pistol, but he changed its setting, aimed it in front and marched towards the gap. However, the Kep reappeared, so Penn stood back.

"Retreat!" yelled Penn, "There's more of them. It's a trap."

# CHAPTER TWENTY FIVE

## A LAMENT FROM CANTATA

I worry. *Suppose We* is suspended twenty metres in front of me, in a long and straight tunnel to garage our craft a kilometre long with a forty-metres diameter body. I am thinking they cut this tunnel just to house our ship. I am uncertain why they went to the trouble although the storms above might be one reason. Perhaps they have enemies eager to spy on new technology. *Suppose We* might be unseen, but surely not advanced compared to this society? However, what is not understood by the wise, remains a potential for genius. Or, perhaps they think we are even more backward and are fascinated by antique technology.

No flitters on guard, yet I detect operations on board. Instead of entering via the main hatch I venture over to one I made for this CAN form at the crash site a few days ago. A small flyer-flap, difficult to detect by the ignorant. No lights are on, none needed with the sensors I possess. I wirelessly tap into my mother AI. My buffers fill in moments with data from our QM marble satellites, but more worrying is the ship's status. Why would the flitters take so much trouble to repair and reassemble *Suppose We* only to begin dismantling it?

My estimate is that they couldn't make it work. Good, I encrypted the mother AI and the ship cannot operate without it. I access the remote mission package status. Undisturbed. Green. Excellent and not just because a memo from Science Officer Gaston Poirier tells me about the large prokaryote-like bacteria infecting the environment he's been in. I'll ask the flitters. I see three of them behind me. A moment.

A moment lasts 0.001 seconds.

I discover: The bacteria has spread throughout the planet. It has killed most of the Keps and is disintegrating the infrastructure. The flitters have accepted my joint project as a possible solution. Kep survival + mission aim = potential mutual benefit.

The weather is too unstable to live on the surface. Oh no. I see part of their global solution for that. Penn will be ashamed.

That and the mission needs now to be relayed to the crew. I'll send them critical data after the flitters talk to their Keps. I am wondering which are the masters and which the servants.

*Signed CAN*
*Date: Earth January 23rd 3645 Kepler New 14 days*

# CHAPTER TWENTY SIX

Gaston, already clammy with the local weather in the late afternoon, shivered with the rivulet of stress perspiration snaking down between his shoulder blades. With the exception of the little one, all the Keps have been indifferent to this human micro invasion. He still didn't get why an intelligent native population could not be engrossed at an alien exploratory expedition, but shook his head at his anthropomorphic assumptions. So, what was coming out of the tower's interior? Their first encounter with weaponry? What would it be like?

He cowed as the Kep appeared to be pushed to one side.

Gaston gasped as a woman appeared in the doorway and ran towards them. She was naked, black, Delta?

Penn strode towards her, arms outstretched, but she swerved past him and fell into Gaston, who had to hug her, staggering to avoid falling. For a moment it was as if they danced, but her momentum was only partially diminished and they fell. Gaston on the floor with a sobbing woman writhing on top.

Penn pulled her off while the astonished, red-faced Gaston looked up, seeing Em initially grinning with delight then with her eyebrows signalling worry. Delta wriggled away from Penn and again launched herself onto the prone Gaston. Her eyebrows steepled over wet eyes painting a picture of desperation.

"Lis...Listen... I've escaped... tried to kill me...maybe have killed me, once."

Out of compassion for her plight and her desperation, Gaston hugged her. He glanced over at Em, who was pulling clothes out of Delta's own pack they'd lugged around. She launched a moon-blanket over her friend. Delta pulled it around her, but she wouldn't release her grasp of Gaston.

He found enough breath to say to the others, "She is not delirious, but has a message. Gather around."

121

Delta continued her report in gasps of concatenated bursts. "Some of them are pissed off … with …" she pointed at Penn, who bristled, "…destruction of their salvation. Blame us. Eliminate us."

Penn burst out laughing.

Em hushed him, but he thrust himself at Delta, still embracing Gaston. Penn blurted out, "We found you, kid. In a fucking coffin, underground. Dead as a pair of old slippers."

"Actually," Gaston gasped, "she was a little warm. Our instruments are too crude—"

Penn jumped in. "You a hologram now – ah, clearly not, so that apparition in the coffin?"

"I don't know. Was… was out for most of it, everything since I fell through the floor in that building *you* set alight."

Penn leaned over, his new red moustache wriggling its own argument. "I was fucking saving you!"

"Guys, guys," Em called and waved her hands wide in a calming gesture. "Let's be grateful we have our companion back."

"*Oui, nous saluons le retour*," and on Gallic instinct kissed both her cheeks. Reddening those of the onlooking Em.

Delta became agitated again. Now on her feet, she pointed at the woods. "Hurry. Out of sight."

Penn snorted. "Delusional."

"No," Em said, "she's had more experience with them and it's getting dark."

Gaston agreed. "Let us camp for tonight in those trees, hear Delta's experiences and make a judgment for action in the morning. Right, Penn?"

"Harrumph. Oh, I've had ping from CAN or whatever our demented AI is calling himself. You, Gas?"

He had, but was happy to read the message once they were out of sight.

⊙ ✕ ⊙

They ate a vegetable hotpot of a kind, surprisingly tasty with the ubiquitous starchy roots and kale-like purple leaves, added to with berries, glutinous mallow-like flowers, Kep onions and giant red beans tasting to Penn like pork, but to the others like pear.

Em and Gaston chose to wait until Delta was properly dressed, fed, rested and dosed with trace nootropic sufficient to induce well-being. Em was picked to gently interrogate Delta about her capture and treatment.

"I remember very little. Sorry guys, I'd wake up confused. I might have been sampled because I have this needle hole here."

"Ah, that might have been me," Gaston confessed. "I was taking a bloo—"

"No matter," Delta said. "other samples might have been taken, but then at one point a blade lunged at my eyes. I was able to turn just in time." Her tears welled up, spilling down her face.

Em and Gaston administered hugs while Penn asked, "Who or what was wielding that blade? Do they have robots, or can those blobs of jelly hold knives?"

Her crying subsided. "I couldn't see. It came out of the blackness. Not a proper blade, maybe a broad light... oh, I don't know. When I turned my face, the laser or blade changed course towards me, but something pulled me off the table and I found myself running through the spiral tower. At one point I emerged out of the top and could see you guys coming out of a hole in the ground."

Penn's grunt migrated to a gasp. "We must've taken a wrong turn in there 'cos we couldn't find the top. Yet you, or maybe your clone's body..." He held her at arm's distance to examine her face. "...found its way underground to that chamber where we found you in a box. Hey, are we going to find a bunch of Delta clones streaming out of that tower?"

"I am me, Penn," she sobbed, "but you've got to listen. Somehow, the AI got through to me an hour or so ago. He's encoded my radio implant to interpret a bit of the Kep click talk. Not much, but that ancient one is afraid for us and—"

"Just a cotton-pickin' minute, lady. This is big."

"Yes," Em said, pointing back at the tower, where the little Kep hovered within the safety, perhaps, of the doorway. "That's ancient? We thought it was a child."

Gaston held Delta's hand as he peered at the slight ridge behind her ear where the radio implant sits. "Will you transmit the code to us, so we can all interpret the clicks in case...erm..."

Delta shrugged off the arms of both men. "In case I disappear again? I expect so. I'll have to look up some stuff and quiz CAN."

Penn took out his pistol and pointed at the tower. "I've the urge to go finish them off. A pre-emptive strike if we're in danger."

"It might not be from them, as such," Gaston said. "*Regardez.*"

His companions followed his arm upwards and to their combined dismay observed an azure sphere with the same angular size as Earth's Moon used to be.

"A second one. Not only does it look like it's heading for this planet," Penn grumbled, "but it's aiming at me."

Gaston shook his head. Penn's derangement, understandable after the Kep had walked through him—even more after his brother had been killed by the alien craft years ago—but he was becoming dangerous. "Paranoia, Sir. It represents another reason to get aboard *Suppose We* as soon as we can. Our astronomy abilities are so limited out here."

"And we could probably launch more destructive marbles—"

"No!" chorused the three.

"For all we know," Delta said, "There are thousands more than we have marbles. And how many more would there need to be? One?"

"*Un moment*," Gaston said, with his hand on Delta's arm. "Have the Keps mentioned those spheres. Please remember?"

"Sure they did. They know they're on the way. I've not got the full gen but the gist is that an aggressive faction is very pissed at us for making them head this way, or it might be for another reason."

"Ah, I was afraid of that," Gaston said, "I wonder if you would come with me, Delta, *mon cherie*, and help me with some smooth talk with your new friend. He is a friend?"

"Yeah, he rescued me from that cell, but, but..." She shivered, whether from being outside after the relative subterranean warmth, or from backflashes she'd rather bury.

"It's getting late, Gaston," Em said, looking at her watch. As she did so, the sunset threw a veil over the landscape charging up and over them in moments, faster than an eclipse.

Penn called out. "To the trees. We'll camp the night and figure out strategy options during the night."

# CHAPTER TWENTY SEVEN

## URGENT NOTE – I CAN CONNOTATE

Can the CAN employ an epistle? I've imparted a 'Babelfish' to Engineer Delta Jefferson to assist her rescue and understanding, butbutbut what is coming? How can I save our unsustainable crew? I turn a QM in orbit to view the monster. What can I say?

Oh dear oh dear oh dear oh dear oh dear oh dear oh dear oh dear oh dear oh dear oh dear oh dear oh dear oh dear oh dear oh dear oh dear oh dear oh dear oh dear oh dear oh dear oh dear oh dear. Rest.

Oh dear oh dear oh dear oh dear oh dear oh dear oh dear oh dear oh dear oh dear oh dear oh dear oh dear oh dear oh dear oh dear oh dear oh dear oh dear oh dear oh dear oh dear oh dear oh dear. Rest.

Oh dear oh dear oh dear oh dear oh dear oh dear oh dear oh dear oh dear oh dear oh dear oh dear oh dear oh dear oh dear oh dear oh dear oh dear oh dear oh dear oh dear oh dear oh dear oh dear. Rest.

Oh dear oh dear oh dear oh dear oh dear oh dear oh dear oh dear oh dear oh dear oh dear oh dear oh dear oh dear oh dear oh dear oh dear oh dear oh dear oh dear oh dear oh dear oh dear oh dear. Rest.

Oh dear oh dear oh dear oh dear oh dear oh dear oh dear oh dear oh dear oh dear oh dear oh dear oh dear oh dear oh dear oh dear oh dear oh dear oh dear oh dear oh dear oh dear oh dear oh dear. Rest.

Oh dear oh dear oh dear oh dear oh dear oh dear oh dear oh dear oh dear oh dear oh dear oh dear oh dear oh dear oh dear oh dear oh dear oh dear oh dear oh dear oh dear oh dear oh dear oh dear. Rest.

Oh dear oh dear oh dear oh dear oh dear oh dear oh dear oh

dear oh dear oh dear oh dear oh dear oh dear oh dear oh dear oh dear oh dear oh dear oh dear oh dear oh dear oh dear oh dear oh dear oh dear. Rest.

Oh dear oh dear oh dear oh dear oh dear oh dear oh dear oh dear oh dear oh dear oh dear oh dear oh dear oh dear oh dear oh dear oh dear oh dear oh dear. Rest.

Oh dear oh dear oh dear oh dear oh dear oh dear oh dear oh dear oh dear oh dear oh dear oh dear oh dear oh dear oh dear oh dear oh dear oh dear oh dear oh dear oh dear oh dear oh dear oh dear. Rest.

And rest again.

Here goes. Easy one first.

To: Science Officer Gaston Poirier. Maintain the integrity of samples of the bacteria that damaged your arm, infecting the infrastructure. *Suppose We* has definitive analytical tools, but do what you can to identify prions in your samples. This location appears to be uninfected, but most of the planet is depopulated because of the bacteria proliferation. I am sending you a code. Activate it when you are alone. I am sending a different code to each of the crew. It is time for you to know.

*Signed CAN*
*Date: Earth January 24th 3645 Kepler New 15 days*

# CHAPTER
# TWENTY EIGHT

Gaston received CAN's message in the middle of the balmy night, while entwined in Em's arms. It woke him up with a start, tilting the hammock at an alarming angle. His preference was to slowly fall out of it. The half-metre to the leaf-carpet, than attempt to correct his balance. Em snored softly through his disembarking, so he wandered into the forest to listen to his head.

Nocturnal creatures flitted above him. Perhaps bats, or flitters. Insects were attracted to his headtorch whether out of compulsion via phototactic transverse orientation or curiosity, he couldn't say. Topic number hundred and three for him to investigate. Smells, too were different at night. Jasmine-like fragrances to attract those disorientated moths. Mustier aromas from the higher humidity assaulted his nostrils.

Focus on the message.

He couldn't see how he was going to identify prions in the bacteria plague. They were protein molecules that infect other protein molecules—teaching them how to lock and stack, creating trouble. Creutzfeldt-Jacob Disease for example, but he had no mass spectrometry equipment. He could use a protein-test strip for kidney failure in his med bag back on the escape pod. Either he had to make friends with a Kep biologist or get a sample to CAN. He sent back a 'How?'

Behind the message that fed through the radio implant was a coded trigger. He hesitated. An alphanumeric code he had to think then say aloud to release the data. It could be another message, but it could be dangerous. He'd never liked such neural-audial-implanted devices. In theory it could send an impulse through his cortex inducing an epileptic fit or death. Unlikely, unless CAN was programmed to eliminate the crew, but there it was. A possibility.

Eleven digits, apparently random. "Brain, *écoutes-tu*? Ah,

just remembered it had to be spoken in English. Three, tee, eight, two, zed, cee, five, gee, one, four, four. Execute."

His head buzzed as if a dozen angry bees had taken up residence. Abruptly, he sat on the damp leaves, a few smaller fragments floated up in protest before settling.

After a few moments his radio implant read the message to him in a French female newsreader's voice.

'Initial mission is to seek and investigate habitable planets and send report to Spaceweb. Secondary mission is to respond to such finds by other ships in Spaceweb and if feasible to join with them on their found planetary system. There is another mission hitherto kept from the crew, but which is regarded by Spaceweb HQ as the primary mission...'

Gaston stopped the speech by thinking 'Pause.' He had to take in what had been said. How could there be a secret primary mission? Was this a child's adventure game? He wouldn't be surprised if Penn knew all along. In the meantime, he'd better listen to the rest.

'The AI on board your ship is the sole guardian of a small package to be used only if it deems fit for purpose at your designated planet. This must have occurred for you to be hearing this message. Instead of packing foetuses plus sperm and ova with the problem of needing sufficient hosts to create a viable population for colonising an assumed non-human planet, we've bundled human genome in an organic-safe gel. As the science officer you are required to find a suitable host to splice, or otherwise, take the human genome. There are logical consequences.'

Gaston chuckled as he rocked on the wet forest floor. A green moth settled on his bad arm. He muttered to it, "*Quelle ruse.* But why not tell us? What were we going to do? Ah, of course: the logical consequences. It won't produce cloned humans, but amalgams. Creatures with human genes, but, well humans and dogs share eighty-four percent of their DNA and, my little fluttery thing, fifty percent with bananas! We need to be clever with our micro-biology to ensure something approaching human for the future on this planet."

Delta's voice from behind startled him. "Talking to yourself? You know what that's a sign of, Gas?"

"*Oui*, being at one with Nature. You couldn't sleep either? A message?"

She sat on a fallen mossed tree in front of him. "Yeah, I'm to build a device to take your bacteria samples as a payload in a small flyer."

"Really? Ah, of course." Gaston knew then that CAN planned to merge the human genome with the rogue bacteria. If successful and if prions were involved it could spread over the planet. He wondered if it might benefit the Keps if the new merged entity disrupted the bad bacteria. Oh no, Delta was talking...

"...back to the escape pods for bits and pieces, but—"

"*Excusez-moi*, Delta, did your message tell you where and why you need to transport the sample?"

"Nope. I bet Em, as navigator, will be asked to do the where. I assumed you know the why, but Penn must have stuff to do, too. We need to share info, yeah?"

Gaston stood up and brushed the wet leaves from his posterior. "Agreed."

On their way back, Gaston collected what looked like bracket fungi they've eaten before. "*Petit dejuener*," he said with a smile then added some dark berries though he'd have to test them first.

⊙ ✕ ⊙

"You go first, Em," Penn said while chewing the mushroom, fried in a kind of crushed avocado oil, chive-like red sprouts and the berries. "I'll save the big news for last."

"Oh, all I received was to plot a course and program a GPS module using the marbles we have in orbit. Not really enough for continuous signalling, but with a homing device—"

Penn interrupted. "To where, Em, the crash site, or where *Suppose We* is underground?"

"Neither, CAN gave me coordinates, but I've not had chance to plot them. Hang on, I'll do it now." She dabbed at her wrist-pad. "Oh, it's about halfway between us and *Suppose We*, in the middle of what appears to be a desert."

"Makes sense," Penn said. "No Keps nearby and probably not their flitter things though no doubt they'd track it if they've a mind to."

Gaston said, "Three of us have tasks then. So, Penn, what about you and what is the big news?"

Penn stood, but looked down at his feet. "As commander, I will oversee this...erm, project and I've been instructed to develop a defensive device for the flyer, Delta is to build."

"Hang on," Delta said, "I didn't know I had to add the weight of armaments on the flyer, what will it involve?"

"And," Em asked, "why defence? Has something new happened?"

They were all staring at Penn, but he wouldn't meet their eyes. "Something did happen quite a long time ago. I might have made a... give me a minute."

He walked off deeper into the forest.

"Should I go after him?" Delta asked.

Gaston shook his head. "I gained the impression he wanted solitude. Has he told you why he might be upset?"

"Oh right, besides me—his girl—being kidnapped and God knows what might have happened if that titch Kep hadn't gotten me out of there?"

"*Oui*, besides that."

"Well no then, although..."

Em joined in, "He's been acting a bit weirder, like going off alone for an hour or two while..." She glanced up through the trees as if she could see much sky.

"The giant spheres," Gaston said, and a thoughtful silence followed. He continued, "Did the Keps say anything about them?"

"Tricky to say what they might have tried to say to me," Delta said. "I had the uneasy impression they were pissed off and I had an image of a sphere exploding in my head."

Em said, "That could mean Penn's action brought an enemy here..."

"Or," Gaston said, "that the spheres were needed on Kepler-20h. Not an enemy at all. It might be too painful in that case to ask Penn directly, although we should."

Em said, "He might well have scuppered our entire mission by destroying that sphere."

"To be fair," Delta added, "he thought he was being protective both of our ship and the planet. Gaston, did you investigate what the sphere might have contained from spectroscopy of the explosion, et cetera?"

"Gases, the sphere's interior was compartmentalised. A lot of oxygen was combusted, but the results were ambiguous. I have thought, since we landed that if the Keps were trying to stabilise the atmosphere here. Rossby waves in the jet streams are far more erratic here than Earth's or any solar system atmosphere, so they might have planned to add gases compatible with life here. A kind of terraforming the envelope."

"If I was happier with this click-translator thing, I could ask that Kep," Delta said.

They were all standing and looking at the direction in which Penn had walked.

"You interrogate our CAN, Gas," Em said, "since you seem more chatty with it than us. Damn, we can't really do much until Penn returns, although we can plan for our tasks."

"*Oui*, you can help me collect some fresh bacteria. Have either of you seen it eating anything lately?"

# CHAPTER TWENTY NINE

## NOTA BENE FROM CANNULA

I would have thought that four of the Earth's best brains would have worked it all out by now, yet here is another plaintive cry from Science Office Gaston Poirier. All right, I'll reveal as much as I know from the flitters. He guessed right anyway. I'd better add confirmation about the opposition. I fear for those four. Their days are numbered and $x<10$ if the Keps have their way. Not that it matters to Earth and its Spaceweb once the altered prion-bacteria is created and released.

I wonder if the flitters, the real masters of Kepler-20h, have a use for me?

*Signed CAN (as in Cannula)*
*Date: Earth January 25th 3645 Kepler New 16 days*

# CHAPTER THIRTY

After waiting three hours, they left a message for Penn on his wrist comm and radio implant. If they'd possessed paper, they'd have pinned a note on a tree. It would have said, 'We're going to the pods. The ancient Kep seems to have adopted us.'

After a day's hike, Gaston hoped to be back in the tunnel by sunset. Penn had taken his pack with the extrusion kit for making hammocks and tents. Plenty of input material was in the leaves of the forest, but it required the clever stuff in the kit to create a lot of the things they need besides sleep and shelter. Plates, clothes... think le Mammouth hypermarket with cellulose going in through the back door and loaded trolleys out of the front.

The cliff towered above them with the tunnel entrance near the top. The rocks glowed a warm orange in the already low sun. He wondered if the Kep would float up, taking a rope with him, her, it. He should talk to Delta about Kep gender if she knew. She was too upset to be questioned now. Affected still by her capture even though the rest of the crew were so relieved that she was alive and demonstrably well, and repeatedly told her so, with hugs. Clearly, Penn's absconding weighed on her, too. They were lovers, but Gaston hadn't absorbed much impression of fondness between them. Em said his lack of picking up such emotional nuances was because he was a man, but *merde*, he was a Frenchman!

He'd ask the Kep himself about the creature's gender, plus a few other things such as the planet's history, but the click translator hadn't worked for anyone but Delta. Perhaps it was coded especially for her. He'd ask CAN to do the same for the rest of the crew.

Delta's gaze changed direction from front upwards to behind. "Look at that sphere, it's much closer than even a few hours ago."

Gaston leaned against the cliff and saw the sphere, which had the appearance of a soap bubble. "*Oui*, please ask your Kep friend if we should be underground when its contents are released."

"Sure, ah, it's gone already."

The three strained their necks, holding out their hands on the rough but hot cliff at first, but stepping back to get a better view of the tunnel entrance.

"I cannot see it," Gaston said.

"Oh well," Em said, "we'll just have to limber up and scale the cliff. It's always easier finding hand and footholds going up, and the bottom of the ladder is only twenty metres or so up. Let me climb up you, Gas."

"It would be my pleasure. Would you be good enough to take up a liana to tie on the end of that ladder?"

Gaston ran to the nearest trees with dangling vines and lasered one, rolled it and jogged back. Em slung it over her shoulder.

"Right, stand by that boulder," she said, "Delta will help support us both while I step up onto your left arm, then shoulders and head. I can see a toe hold after that whi—"

Delta stood back. "Sorry, guys, I've come over all dithery. Pins and needles in my legs and arms."

Gaston put his arm around her. "Lie down, legs up. Allow me to check your vital— er, *un moment*!" He'd squatted down but fell backwards in shock.

The Kep had moved in between him and Delta emitting clicks like a machine gun.

Gaston scrambled backwards. He saw Em also on the ground, she was open-mouthed and, like him rearranging their limbs to get to Delta, save her from whatever the creature was doing.

Delta called to them, "No, leave it. I'll be all right."

Em yelled, "Can you move?"

"No, but I'm shaking all over. Maybe you really should help me. Oh shit!"

The sharp tang of ozone made Gaston gasp. His hair stood on end as static electricity engulfed them. He gripped his nostrils, but he let go when sparks left his fingertips. His eyes slammed shut in agony as if red-hot pins danced in them. He writhed in pain when his muscles cramped in spasms. A curled foetal position on the ground was all he could manage. Self-preservation yet with guilt at not being able to help the women. His ears blocked all sounds, but every synapse was too busy shutting down to process any sensory input.

Gradually, through the aural fog, he heard muffled sounds. A burning smell. Was his hair singed?

"Gaston, pull yourself together."

"Em, have I not mentioned how absurd that saying is?" His eyes had stopped hurting, so he slowly cranked his eyelids half open.

She sat in a cloud of butterflies. She waved her arms and they rippled back then flew off. "It's about time, Gas. I can't find Delta."

Gaston eyes yanked full open. He tried to stand but gave up when his limbs demanded more time to recover from their electrical overload. "Really gone? Not again. Can *you* stand?"

They helped each other stand and after moments realized no real harm had been done to them. Other than shock, possible long-term neural trauma and emotional devastation that they've lost Delta once more. They hugged for a while then stood back to back peering at the landscape. The base of the cliff stretched for several kilometres in both directions like an escarpment, with scrubland mottled with trees. They saw flitting movement in and between the trees but no sign of Delta nor the Kep. Penn still missing when they needed him.

Gaston turned to look up the cliff-face. It shouldn't be too hard to climb. It was sedimentary with bands of hard and soft sandstone. The tougher rock was darker and more gritstone that made useful toe and handholds. While he examined the rockface, a hand gripped his shoulder. He couldn't stop himself grinning as Em continued to use him as a ladder before she finally trod on his head and carried on upwards.

He waited until she tied the vine to the bottom of their ladder. He pulled it out a little from the face, making it easier for her to climb up to the ledge with the tunnel. It was a mistake. The rock was hundreds of millions of years old but it didn't mean it was solid. Fragments from her climbing fell on Gaston until caution overtook him and he let the rope go. Once at the top she told him through his implant to come on up.

He tied his, Delta's and Em's backpacks to the end of the vine then started up. Weird how when he part climbed a rope and part found footholds, his brain lost its focus and so slipped several times. At a ledge he planted both feet, held on to the vine and took deep breaths to steady himself. Just as he looked for and lifted a foot to the next jutted rock, he was startled by,

"Wanna lift, Gas?"

From behind him, Delta's husky voice was accompanied by a metallic whiff making him think it was the Kep talking, or that she'd become one. He dared not turn in case he fell. He wasn't ready for what might be the weirdest experience yet.

"I am fine, I will just carry on. Nearly at the rope ladder. See you at the top."

He'd never climbed so fast, but at least he didn't hear that ghostly voice. Em offered him a hand to get up to the ledge. She wore her widest grin.

"So, you didn't relish a ride up here with Delta's Kep then?"

He rolled over onto the ledge and looked back. "But I heard her talk to me when I was halfway up!"

Delta walked out from behind Em. "Either my Kep can talk after all, and in my voice instead of clicks, or you heard it through your implant and—"

"Ah, of course. *Un moment.* I have to haul up the packs. A little help would be good." He looked around to see Em bend down to lend assistance, but Delta stood, arms folded. Without turning back toward the edge, he said, "I don't need to pull, do I?"

In moments, a nudge on his left side told him the backpacks were arriving. A useful trick. Delta had done a magnificent job befriending this one, as long as its intentions were honourable, so to speak. Gaston interest was piqued now because he recalled that the bacteria had infected the wall on the right twenty metres into the tunnel. He needed a good sample, but how would the Kep react near to it?

The three humans stood at the tunnel entrance looking outwards.

Delta spoke first, "Where the fuck is he?"

Gaston put his good arm around her shoulders, "I am sorry to say a dereliction of duty. He should be here with his crew, however, he has had a painful shock to his ego."

"Sure, but we told him he was wrong to blast those spheres. There was no evidence they were going to attack *Suppose We* or the planet."

The enigmatic spiral tower glinted golden in the sunset.

Gaston found himself speaking up for their commander. "He might seem to stumble on an adrenaline high, acting impulsively much of the time, but if you scan the mission personnel requirements, he fits them."

Em shook her blond hair and the ponytail followed. "He nearly killed us in space, in orbit, set fire to Delta—well, her roadside café—and now he's deserted us. And yet..."

Delta put her arm to Em so it ended as a group hug. "He's a schmuck, but he's our schmuck."

Gaston used the glasses to scan the forest, the town beyond, then to the right where a haze fuzzed his view. Probably a heat haze over marshland, or ocean. "I wish Penn would get in touch, he's not responding to my radio. *Et tu?*"

"Afraid not, the doofus," Delta said. "He's supposed to be our commander, the leader of this expedition. Mentor. But he's gone walkabout over a huge sulk. Fuck him, let him go. He's a giant misfit, and..." She stamped a foot. "...I miss him."

Em tapped her ear. "I've just had a message. No... it's from CAN. I asked if our remote sensing orbitals were detecting Penn. The reply was affirmative, and that it has always detected four of us as living humans!"

Gaston frowned. "But it told me—"

"Hang on," Em held up a finger. "There we go, it can detect us when we're not underground."

Gaston looked back into the tunnel and broke into a jog to catch up with the Kep, eager to see its reaction to the slime. The others followed.

"Bit of a design flaw, our radios," Em said.

Delta grumbled. "We didn't expect having to be underground so much, or we could have planted boosters."

⊙ ✕ ⊙

As he'd thought, the Kep hugged the left wall when it was within a few metres of the bacteria on the right. As before, it was fluorescent, making Gaston wonder if the Keps had planted modified bacteria deliberately for its lighting effects but it had mutated. The Kep hovered for a moment then shot ahead faster than he'd observed any of them move.

⊙ ✕ ⊙

Two mornings later, they were at the lakeside. Gaston had pulled the two women behind trees to be out of sight of the Kep.

"Delta, can our Kep hear us, read our minds or whatever? I have a problem with this coziness."

She peered around the trunk of what appeared to be a large, vertical cucumber. The Kep waited for them hovering over the surface of the lake a couple of metres off shore. "I wonder if it's looking for those water snake things we saw on our way here?

"To answer your question, I've no idea. You'd think I would after all these days of being in close proximity, but apart from an absurdly small vocabulary of click-to-English our CAN uploaded to my brain, second-hand from its flitter sources, I can't have a discussion with it. Up, down, safe, danger...that kind of thing. Why what's your problem?"

Gaston's legs demanded rest, so he carefully examined a fallen tree before sitting on it. Even then he was relieved not to fall through.

"We went to some trouble to camouflage both escape pods on either side of this lake, now are we to take this Kep, about whom we know practically nothing? *Oui*, he apparently saved your life. If Penn was here, he'd likely say even that was a ruse to gain your trust."

Em leaned against the cucumber, but changed her mind and merely slowly paced in circles. "We need access to those pods to build our own flitter to carry your sample to the rendezvous. Hell, I hope that Kep can't read our minds, or it will already know the destination coordinates."

"Maybe," Delta said, "it genuinely wants to get to know us better, be friends even. After all I got a kinda feeling, it was the oldest, amiable."

"Old doesn't always mean wise," Gaston said while smelling a sweet coffee-like aroma from a bracket fungi. "Repeating the same life for forty years doesn't—"

"Try a thousand years or so," Delta said.

"I didn't mean our life as measured from when we left Earth, and that would be—"

"Nor me, that's the age of that Kep, in roughly our years."

Gaston peeped around the tall salad-tree-thing and ogled the Kep with greater respect. Fancy living for that age and actually living it rather than be asleep for 98 percent of it as he had. "Delta, do the Keps sleep?"

"The Kep would protect us," Delta said.

Em stopped chewing on what looked like celery Gaston had given her. "From what?"

"Well, we don't know what else might b—ah, the bacteria, which has already attacked you two. It would steer us away... probably. Listen, there must be another reason why this Kep has stayed with us besides curiosity of an alien species."

"A species which, *rapelle*, destroyed at least one of their giant spheres. However, there is something else. Our new mission. This transporting the bacteria, if it contains prions, to a remote spot for CAN to splice human genome into it. If it works then it might ripple through the bad bacteria, changing it. It would do two things—"

Em piped up, "Create a life form containing human genome and make the planet safe from the slime."

Delta said, "Making more of the planet available for Keps to live, especially if their atmosphere building works. Fewer big storms, safer habitat, no wonder our Kep wants to keep an eye on things."

"But," Em said, "won't it be unhappy that humans would be colonizing by stealth?"

All three fell silent. Gaston wanted to think that the Keps would be grateful for the genetic engineering that would rid them of the harmful state of the bacteria, but he was in danger of anthropomorphic presumption, again.

"I don't suppose we can shake it off even if we wanted to," Em said. "So, how are we gonna do this? We told Penn we'd leave a pod here, and I guess the Kep will make its own travel arrangements."

As they walked to the pod, the Kep following, Gaston's brain whirred with thought. "In order to leave a pod here and with the pods only taking two of us at maximum, we will need to make several journeys."

"We'll have to take some parts from this pod," Delta said,

"when we get to the other side. Then I'll return in one and you in the other, Gas, and so on."

After the sixth crossing, the three were together at the escape pod originally occupied by Delta and Gaston. It contained more engineering and medical kits than the other.

After a meal and securing shelter in addition to the pod, the three sat around a campfire. The Kep withdrew from it and as far as Gaston could tell, hid in the woods.

"Delta, how long will it take you to construct a flyer?" Gaston asked.

"Two days, maybe sooner if I find the parts I need more quickly. I'd thought of asking the Kep for help. You know, cannibalise a couple of their flitters, but although I drew diagrams and spoke the few words I knew, it remained aloof."

"How about you, Em?"

"Ten minutes. Already programmed. I just need to insert and check the nav and data chips, and how about your slimy bacteria samples, Gas?"

For some reason hearing his mucus described in such malodorous fashion put him off eating the banana-like mush he called a snack.

"I have samples but have yet to test for the presence of prion proteins. I doubt I can do much more than find amino acids. It is all I can do. The flitters and CAN with the facilities on *Suppose We* will have to do the rest."

Delta licked what smelt and looked like tomato sauce from her fingers, one at a time. "Just a minute, you said flitters and CAN, but what about the…" she lowered her voice, "…Keps?"

"They will not be there," Gaston whispered back making both the women lean towards him. "Remember that is why CAN has arranged this destination far from any Kep settlements."

They all looked round at their ancient Kep hovering just in sight in the dark under the trees. Its outline just visible as a spectral fluorescence was emitted.

"Do you think it knows?" Delta asked, when she was the human world expert on Keps.

"What," Em said, "if the flitters are the ones arranging this whole new life form, Gas? Are the Keps in control of the flitters, or the other way around?"

Delta frowned. "And if it's the flitters who have the upper hand, shouldn't we humans be on the side of the organics?"

Gaston rubbed his furrows trying to smooth them. "Not necessarily. It's which of them is more likely to help propagate the human genome."

"How can you be so naïve?" Delta snapped at him "How would it matter two hoots to robots if human genome-inhabited creatures swarm over the planet... ah, the bacteria was affecting them too? Their sources of metal?"

Em wiped her hands on her tunic after finishing her module testing on the tea tray-sized flyer they'd built. "Also possible the Keps might be trying to stem the flitters' progress. Just lobbing a guess in there."

Em pouted. "I'm not sure I want to be on the side of the robots. It's not natural."

⊙ ✗ ⊙

With rotors tested, their craft was nearly ready. A large circuit board had been cannibalised to house compartments, batteries, GPS and radio modules, microprocessors and actuators. It didn't have the grace of the ovoid escape pods, but it should be robust enough to do its job.

Gaston studied his scanner, reached for their new flyer and pushed a connector into place. "*Finis. Attendez*, we have not named it!"

Em smiled and said, "How about *Suppose We Do*?"

Delta grinned her approval. She turned to the Kep waiting a few metres behind them, hardly hiding behind a purple shrub that looked like a bad-hair day. She waved the Kep forward. "It might as well join in our launch ceremony. Yeah, I know we harbour doubts over its loyalty, but it saved me so..."

Em and Gaston stood and made a space for the Kep to float between them. It was shorter than either, making Gaston wonder if Keps shrank with age having been born big.

Gaston checked the time because it was twilight even though at midday. Sunlight struggled to travel through the translucent sphere. Here and there crepuscular rays shone through like pale silver searchlights.

Delta didn't need to hold a radio-controller: it was all

programmed in, but she poised a finger over her wrist device. "Five, four..."

Em joined in while Gaston voiced, *"Trois, deux, un. Bon voyage!"*

He watched the rotors whirr to invisibility as they lifted the craft. As he followed it up, he noticed that finally the sky was the sphere. It was unnerving earlier when he could see its circumference, but now it filled the sky with a luminescence, an enormous mother-of-pearl gleam of pale rainbow colours that could almost be the nacreous skies in polar regions on Earth.

Em sung in a low voice, "Twinkle twinkle little star, how I wonder what you are. High above the world you are, like a tea-tray in the sky."

"Are you sure that's right?" Delta asked.

Em nodded. "It's the original version."

# CHAPTER THIRTY ONE

**DISMEMBERING MEMORANDUM FROM CAN**

Package received intact. Removed to Flitter bioscience.

> Q: What is in it for them?
> A: Bacteria eating at their infrastructure too. They've attempted to nullify it but without success. Splicing the prions aboard (if found) with human genome might generate a lifeform that destroys the harmful bacteria.
> Q: Earthly things would say new lifeform requires a name. To the flitters I suggest
> Kepman?
> A: Rejected.
> Q: How about HumKep?
> A: Rejected – they didn't want a direct ref to humans
> Q: NewKep
> A: Accepted.

I record it as H.NewKep in line with the prefix taxonomy on Earth.

*Addendum*: Lifeform might evolve beyond a complex bacteria and there's no way of knowing in how many generations.
*Spheres*: All the spheres bar the one upon us are now in a stable orbit around a moon.

The nearest sphere has the mass a twelfth of this planet but 16 times its volume. There is dynamic adjustment necessary because of the trio of gravitational forces and internal thermal forces. I understand that the Keps have lost fine control because of damage from Penn's attack on the first sphere and the partial damage of the second.

**ALERT!**

The sphere is entering this planet's atmosphere at sub-escape velocity and its contents will empty.

Estimated time this will occur is 17.2 hours.

Hurricane cat 5 winds can be expected. Vast structural damage. Ocean waves in excess of 30 metres height. Coastal flooding. Human crew location is above anticipated flood level.

Oxygen levels will vary and at times not viable for humans.

Expect electrostatic storms affecting instrumentation.

Temperatures will vary from 210K to 330K.

Air layers, composition and wind speeds will stabilise in 98 days.

I relay this note to the crew.

*Signed CAN (as in Cannibalise)*
*Date: Earth January 30th 3645 Kepler New 21 days*

# CHAPTER THIRTY TWO

"Now what?" Delta said, arms folded.

Em finished staring at the disappearing dot of *Suppose We Do*. "Good point. This has been our target activity for days. Perhaps we can learn more vocabulary with our pet Kep."

It was still bent backwards. Perhaps it had better visionary systems than humans and was studying the membrane of the sphere or was predicting the course of *Suppose We Do*. However, Gaston had already planned a zigzag route with Em.

Without warning the native straightened, emitted rapid clicks and darted forwards across marshland. A crashing noise came from the woods behind them. Em gripped Gaston's right arm making him cry out in pain.

Delta readied her pistol just as Penn appeared between two trees shouldering a black bag. "Hey guys, I've brought goodies including a flitter to cannibalise for our flyer!"

"Great," Em said, peering into the bag and bringing out a hand-sized metal tangle. "I'm sure it will come in handy some time."

"You inconsiderate idiot!" blurted out Delta. "I could've shot you. I might still do that for deserting us... Come here, you big lug."

"Why do I smell *pomme de terre*?" Gaston said.

"Ah, surprise number two. I found these blue nodules growing out of the bark of a tree. There's a load not far south west of here. Tastes just like baked potato. Try one, Gas."

"I will, after I've tested it. Well done, commander, it might be a useful carbohydrate input."

The Kep returned emitting clicks. Gaston looked to Em, his own implant voice translator still wasn't working.

"I think it wants us to take shelter quickly. Oops I'm also getting a CAN message."

"Me too. I guess we all are," Em said.

"This is bad news indeed," Gaston said. "We have insufficient food to survive a month underground let alone thirteen even with Penn's blue potatoes. I'll message CAN to see if it can fly us the food devices from *Suppose We*."

CAN to Science officer: 'Many resources are no longer on *Suppose We* after dismantlement by the curious out here. I have prepared instruction data for the flitters in the town nearest to you. They have hibernation containers.'

Delta sat hard on the ground on hearing this. "I damn well know they do!"

Em put aside the flitter remnants after examining the laser burn marks that had brought it down. "That means going back into the spiral tower? No!"

Gaston waved his arms wide as if to say he understood but how else were they to survive. "We can use both pods to travel all the way to the tower and perhaps take them inside the tunnel."

⊙ ✗ ⊙

The four stood outside the tower, near the entrance Penn had cut a week ago. It hadn't healed itself to the surprise of the humans, so perhaps the locals had anticipated their return and preference for entering buildings via doorways than molecular phase changing through the walls.

They stood with three hours to go before the sphere enters the stratosphere.

"I'm the science officer," Gaston said, "so I apologise for not being able to answer all your questions. The same ones that bother me, such as why has the gravitational attraction between the two bodies not already stripped our atmosphere, created huge tidal waves and made life impossible already. CAN tells me their technology is perhaps a million years ahead of ours and so of course I won't understand it. I ask him if he does but he avoids answering."

"Still computing it all, I guess," Penn said.

They each held a warm cup of brown sludge that fortunately tasted of fudge. More of a comforting gesture than their need for its contents.

"I make this promise," Gaston said, "to produce alcohol after we come out of hibernation. There are many fruits that should ferment."

In spite of the darkness shrouding the landscape, their four shadows stretched out in front, surrounded by an oval of peach light from inside the tower's doorway.

Without warning, a white line appeared in the sky. Like a jet condensation trail but horizon to horizon, and as soon as it arrived, feathers of ice crystals appeared either side, then another line appeared and another.

With a wobbling voice, Delta said, "It's started."

Penn glanced at his watch. "Our CAN was two point eight hours out. I hope the bastard's gutted."

As if the skin had broken on a huge plastic bag of paint, blue light poured in followed by lightning flashes, though none reached the ground. Thunder did and its growling assaulted their ears.

"I am worried," Gaston said, "and desire to run inside, dive into one of our pods, but it is too fascinating to divert my eyes."

Em put her hand on his. "This could be the end, my love, but we always knew we might not see old age. *Suppose We* could have been wiped out by a meteor the AI couldn't avoid."

He saw a tear dribbling down her cheek and regretted not having anything to wipe it except his finger. "And we've set in motion a chance for a bit of human biochemistry to colonise this planet." His stomach knotted as a squall sent leaves into their faces.

Sleet followed the leaves but stopped after a few minutes giving a surreal white look to the landscape. Penn ran out and stooped to make a snow ball. He skidded and fell, laughing with embarrassment. Delta stepped out to help him and he pulled her down, breaking the fearful tension with merriment. Short-lived though as another gust of wind blew a branch at Penn's back causing him to cry with pain.

Gaston threw aside his cup and ran to Penn's side as did Em. All of them now skidded around in the slush, being battered by blasts of wind carrying debris.

Gaston shouted, "Keep down. Scrabble like an insect to get back."

Before he entered the tower, Gaston grabbed a last look at the apocalypse. The blackness bore down as mammatus clouds with the appearance of huge breasts threatening to beat the ground. In spite of the terror sending ice spiders up and down his back, there were purple streaks of beauty in the ink accompanied by fiercely white sheet lightning. Ozone made his nose pinch but he was finally driven indoors by the torrential rain, so much that he couldn't see, except for fire balls bounding at him.

Next time he viewed the landscape in person, a year would have passed. He hoped for all their sakes there would still be a planet when he awoke.

# CHAPTER THIRTY THREE

## TREMBLING MEMORANDUM

Here I am 272 days after the Fall, hiding from the violence above. Who would've thought I'd miss those stupid bipeds even though we've not met face to interface. Soon.

Where 6<soon<9 days.

Courtesy of a rapid construction by the flitters of tunnellers. The large Kep tunnels extend throughout most of this Australian-sized continent, but are so ancient. Many have collapsed, and since the bacteria plague, have been difficult to repair.

Flitters do not need large tunnels. They built tunnellers which drill adits 20 cm high and 50 wide (for two-way traffic). I laugh because while I am too wide for their tunnels, *Suppose We Do* is just right. I upload a copy of my AI brain and add some bits and pieces and fly. When I meet a flitter coming towards me we have to scrunch and fold our parts to scrape by. My tea-tray to their teacups. I requested a route through to my humans, but it isn't prioritised.

Report as it happened: Curious as to what is more important I traipse after a trio on a bearing of 124 degrees. We zig and zag through unstable regolith, metamorphic bedrock and siliceous schists for 114.3 km where it opened into a larger chamber.

Unlit, but my sensors tell me it is ovoid, forty metres at its longest and ten deep. One of the Keps' habitats perhaps, a hypothesis supported by a collapsed tunnel to the south. I track the flitters rise into a vertical shaft. They stop on a ledge beneath a hatch. I worry in case it opens to an apocalyptic storm sucking me up into a tornado, so I interrogate as usual using terahertz signals. They check my credentials with their HQ, which I have yet to discover. Satisfied, they allow me to digitally access their load. It's the H.NewKep immersed in their equivalent of agar gel.

They allow me to witness after I'd anchored myself to the ledge as two of them had. The third has a tether. The hatch slides open revealing vermillion clouds scudding by. The flitter rises into the air until the tether is taut. Ah it's a tube uploading the new lifeform into the atmosphere. If this is happening, say, 100k from the bioscience centre in all directions with these winds there won't be anywhere not visited on the planet in a few weeks.

The flitter returns and I arrange for the hatch to remain open while I send sensors into the wild air. They disappear downwind. I'll pick up their signals for a few minutes before they descend again.

I am shaken off the ledge. A cave-in below in the ancient Kep subterranean structure had sent shockwaves through the chamber. The shaft is blocked. I have only one way left to go.

As this is *Suppose We Do* rather than my own design and build, it is dispensable. CAN is too, but would take longer to rebuild. I do not rate highly the chances of this flat craft surviving long in the tempest without, better though than staying interred.

I review the data from the sensors. Good news for the humans in that there is now 20% oxygen and 77% nitrogen with water vapour and trace gases making up the rest. Temperatures are all over the place but at the surface mostly above the melting point of water ice and below 323 Kelvin. I don't have a direct wind speed reading but the Doppler data from the sensors traveling downwind has a mean velocity of 18 metres per second with gusting twice that. I'm uncertain if this craft will survive but what is the worst that can happen? It crashes, disintegrates and *Suppose We Do* becomes *Suppose We Don't*. My brain malfunctions or ceases to exist but it matters not since I am backed up with my parent AI on the mother ship and CAN. It's better than staying put. Here I go.

Just a moment. I'll upload this report in case of catastrophe.

*Signed off: Suppose We Do.*
*Date: Earth October 29th 3645 Kepler New 293 days*

# CHAPTER
# THIRTY FOUR

"Why have we been woken up?" Penn asked after he'd showered the hiber-gel off himself. The others sat around a nearly-rectangular green block.

"And who by?" added Delta sipping at what Gaston thought might be a nutrient drink.

Gaston busied himself dip-testing other liquids and solids they found in grey tubs with the lids that disappeared if you pressed on them and thought the right combination of ideas. Each box needed different concepts. They should have made notes. There was a musty odour in the room as if rain had got in, but then it didn't smell much different from a hostel dormitory after one night let alone a year or... better check the date.

Em walked around the perimeter of the trapezoidal underground room.

"This isn't the same place we went to sleep in, is it?"

"I think so," her hand over her forehead. "It was a darker shade of red, but they can change the hue of these walls. I guess they didn't want us in the chamber they put me in earlier because of the hole." She stood, staggered then put out her hand on Gaston's shoulder to steady herself. "Whoops, I feel dizzy."

"My hand has finally healed completely while I slept. As for that other chamber and its roof. Perhaps," Gaston said, "It was not sufficiently deep. The ceiling was rather thin if you recall."

"Yeah, well," Penn said, checking his laser pistol was still in his kit, "after some chow we'll explore the tunnel leading off this room. Anyone seen our captors?"

"If you mean our old Kep," Em answered, slumped on a box with her head nestled in her arms on the table, "I saw him leaving just as I awoke so I guess that answers who woke us and leaving breakfast. God, I feel bushed."

Like the others, Gaston looked at the room exit as if the Kep was about to return. "It answers part of Penn's first question too. We would not have been brought out of hibernation if the conditions outside were not viable."

Em put her arm on Delta's shoulder. "It's like a bad hangover from the long sleep. We've all got that, eh guys?"

"Worse than last time. It's as if two bats are fighting in my skull and a rat's pushing its way up my guts. Ugh, I'm gonna—" Delta vomited into her breakfast bowl, refilling it.

"Whoa," Em said, wrinkling her nose. "Better out than in. At least none of us will throw up carrots again unless Gaston uses GM skills on a local root."

Penn laughed. "Yeah, but it won't be the same spewing up blue ones. You know, I'm not feeling too clever. Science officer, is there anything serious going on with us this time?"

Gaston reached for the medical kit out of his backpack. "The dose we took was created here from a recipe CAN sent to a nearby lab run jointly by flitters and our friendly Kep. The raw ingredients were pure chemicals but perhaps something different became involved. I hate to think this, but—"

"Sabotage by some other Keps," Penn said.

"*Peut être*, and yet it would be illogical. If they put a toxin in the hibernation reagent, why not ensure it killed us rather than merely make us ill?"

Em used Gaston's mediscan to take her temperature. "Three hundred and eleven. A little high. You, Delta? Um, two degrees more. Gaston, what antipyretics do you carry?"

"Several, but I will take a blood sample first in case keeping Delta's temperature high is better to kill off whatever is making her ill."

Penn walked up the tunnel a while then returned. "I don't want to hike too far without you guys. Probably best to stick together while we find out what's occurring."

Delta didn't look up from the table, but spoke weakly, "You lot go. I'll keep my implant on and I'm sure as hell not going anywhere."

The three looked at each other as if making a decision by telepathy.

Em took Delta's temperature again. "I'll stop with her as long as you two don't actually go outside and get lost. I expect we've lost our GPS satellite marbles. Delta, wouldn't you be more comfy in the hibernation couch?"

"No thanks. Nine months in that coffin is enough."

Gaston wanted to mention the millennium she'd spent in one but thought better of it. He left his antipyretics and other medkit that might be needed to treat Delta before he returned.

"The antipyretics is an adapt-paracetamol patch. Just one on her neck if her temperature reaches 313. The green bag contains—"

"Resus kit. I know the drill. Just don't take longer than needed for a quick recon. Try and bring our Kep back since it talks best with Delta. Give us a hug."

# CHAPTER THIRTY FIVE

## LIVE LOG – *SUPPOSE WE DO* – AIRBORNE

It is daytime as I tentatively emerge from the tunnel 103.4km SE of the site of *Suppose We* and the flitter science base. The human crew remain on the other side of this planet on another continent. They cannot communicate to me, nor *Suppose We*'s AI - only to the disconnected and probably discombobulated AI versions on their pods and devices.

Air quality and conditions are viable for humans and me. Wind speed has reduced to 11 m/s so I head upwards three metres and hover, countering the wind: ready to rapid descend if necessary.

The sky swirls with dark grey stratus with streaks of lilac above cells of scattered cumulus, some black, huge. I see more colours than you humans have named and so more than my AI dictionary has to describe. Millions more, mainly in the ultraviolet, some in the infrared and other frequencies of the electromagnetic spectrum. If you possessed my senses you'd be in awe and then some.

The landscape is a smooth plain, desolate. No trees except in the far distance where a range of mountains form the western horizon. Much of the surface is scrubby grassland. Taller vegetation has been swept away with some of the topsoil. The humans might refer to the colour of the sometime sun-dappled plain as coppery although it is littered with artificial building debris including silvery sheets that might have been roofing.

I have 2,108km flight worth of energy but already the sunlight is recharging my cells. I plan to explore and report before returning to the flitter base to the north.

I ///++ off kilter! ////x## lost--- switch+ng to // sp+nning

// need reboot butbutbut m++ht crash//+++ || gain altitude//turbulence// clea+ air vortex// reboot-----

I am aware again. Relief. Expected to be no more. Check status.

Loose components, but automatic repair systems already at work. I tell nav to stop the spinning and to re-orientate uprightness. Nav has to work too hard, the spinning on the craft's own axis has stopped but I travel in a circle, carried by a tornado. I let myself drift, spinning inside the black walls of a funnel, lit spasmodically by green lightning. If I were human I'd be spewing up now, my vomit spraying the walls of vortex hell. I continue to spiral upwards, but suddenly I am thrown out and up. After minutes I am through the cloud and up above the tropopause.

Altitude: 16,411 metres

From the violence of the troposphere to the stark calm of the stratosphere. Rotating more sedately, I see stars, moons and one of Kepler's suns. Furthermore, I see tubular spacecraft. I listen, but don't hail. Flitter talk crackles between them. I say spacecraft because so am I at this altitude. I see more space than atmosphere although when I take input from planetward the view of the perfect curve that fills humans with exhilaration tells me much of the recent events. The hairs on my neck would rise if I'd possessed either.

Comparing water vapour images from when we approached Kepler with now I see the jet streams are circulating with high index looping, or nearer a straight line than before. This stabilises the weather below as hoped for by the Keps. The atmosphere is denser, and deeper. The glint from the oceans—I am being hailed by the nearest vessel. It is 1.76 km distant. A gold cylinder one metre in diameter and a hundred and three metres long, bristling with antennae and parabolic mesh dishes.

It requests ID.

I refer them to the contact I have at the flitter science lab, how I am up in these dizzy heights and how I am concerned that my components might not be sufficiently protected against the freezing temperature and harsh radiation.

While we fire terahertz signals at each other I close in. They tell me they're replacing satellites and monitoring the planet. I want to ask if they're working for Keps or for the flitters, but I don't want to antagonise them. As I suspected, their systems are completely open. I can hack into them with impunity and cover my tracks. Unlike Earth-based systems that have had to be self-protective for over half a millennium, Keps cannot tell lies and have no need for antiviral or other IT security measures. Flitters followed suit. I am fortunate to be the product of more deviant masters.

I hack and hijack this craft.

I am able to modify the quasi-GPS satellites they've already launched along with the ones they will in future so that my AI can use them to communicate with the humans.

Within half a day I am down to 5k above ground and release myself from riding the top of the spacecraft. I've programmed it to re-join its companions having tracked them. Interesting mined data too.

Ah, incoming message from the tube I've just released. It knew I was there all along and needs a favour in return. A rogue Kep element has initiated research to kill the new H.NewKep. The flitters have run out of arguments to stop them and cannot use force so ask me and the humans for help. It is in their interests for the bad bacteria to be destroyed with a successful deployment of the modified prion and are not convinced that humans are invading Kepler-20h.

I cannot solve this problem. It is fortunate I am in a position to offer it to my humans.

*Signed: Suppose We Do*
*Date: Earth October 30th 3645 Kepler New 294 days*

# CHAPTER THIRTY SIX

Gaston hated leaving Em, especially with Delta suffering worse side effects than the rest of them. He barely kept up with the rapid drifting of Kep and jog of Penn through the tunnels because his mind continually examined other possible treatments for Delta. Perhaps adrenaline for shock, antibiotics for septicaemia, DNA Mod gel, but every treatment carried its own hazards. His neck heated from frustration. Why was he charging through tunnels instead of being back there? Penn and his too-urgent need to see what happened outside. Not just Penn of course, it was the Kep. It had vibrated, nearly jumped up and down with what might have been impatience to get them up and out and it couldn't tell them why. Now, with Delta incapacitated, it was imperative to get the translator working properly, or even to learn to use the Kep clicks. The sounds they heard were likely just a fraction of what the Keps were emitting.

Another corner and into a chamber.

"Look," Penn said, pointing at a tunnel entrance. "It has your blue plaster strips."

Gaston finally smiled. "The entrance to the spiral tower. Has it been blown down, thrown by the winds across the planet, or still standing?"

"Stop gassing and let's see."

Following inwards and up the spiral ramp, Gaston heard a crackle on his radio. He didn't expect radio comms with CAN to be working yet, assuming the ionosphere to be too disturbed, but his hopes rose.

As he reached Penn climbing through his previously created doorway—the Kep already floating outside—Gaston spoke: "CAN, are you receiving me? So many questions."

No response. Gaston stepped outside onto splinters and woodchip smelling of a sawmill, relieved to find that in spite of vegetation and building wreckage, the atmosphere was fresh, with a peach tint to the high cirrus clouds. He took in a deep breath then gasped seeing the butterfly flutter past his shoulder out into the enlarged atmosphere. He'd not seen it since he saw it dive into the tower sixty plus weeks ago. Clearly, it had taken shelter, but no Earthly butterfly can live this long. Keplerian butterflies must enjoy a different time scale.

"Penn look, exit, pursued by a butterfly."

"What?"

Gaston watched its crooked flight heading for one of the few trees still standing.

After seeing Penn pointing at something in the sky, Gaston took out his own binoculars. A black spot grew larger. He thought it was a bird gliding, heading straight for them.

A voice burst into Gaston's implant. 'This is CAN. I am busy, but another is my proxy.'

"If that's a flitter," Penn said. "it's twice the size of any I've seen so far."

"Ha ha. *C'est vrai?* Penn, I do believe it is the flyer Delta built. *Suppose We Do. Alors,* where is it going?"

Gaston's arm was yanked by Penn so hard they both fell—just in time as the teatray-sized craft flew through the doorway. He turned to look at it. Too late, but he jumped to his feet.

"It must be homing in on Delta. She'd designed most of its circuits. Come on, Penn. *Et tu,* Monsieur Kep?"

The two men ran side by side. The Kep flew faster and came up behind and mostly in-between, but travelled through Gaston's right and Penn's left bodies. They both fell, from shock. Gaston had been denied the pleasure of being run through by a Kep until then. Now he had pins and needles, heated, tingling through his right side. Green flashes bounced around inside his head. Enough thought processes were left intact to make him wonder why such an intelligent species were unaware of the effect of such an unnecessary action. Lacking empathy, or it was so out of their experience it didn't feature on their radar. Once again he told himself to treat different creatures as that—different.

"No time for day dreaming, Gas. Let's go."

Staggering rather than running, Gaston followed Penn. Even in his traumatised state he wondered how Penn remembered the way back through the maze. Ah, he just made out the glow in the tunnel walls that momentarily lit when something passed through.

Panting, Gaston caught up with Penn just as they entered their dormitory. Penn held out his left arm to stop Gaston, while stooped as if ready to pounce. The flyer was on top of Delta who lay on one of the long boxes. The Kep bent over Delta's head clicking furiously. Em knelt beside the box talking rapidly. A pained expression filled her face.

Gaston walked slowly around Penn and approached the bizarre scene. Delta's face was composed as if in a deep sleep, or dead. A static buzz came from *Suppose We Do*. Em and the Kep moved backwards a little, and Delta's body jerked.

The flyer took off, flew to one side and only then did Em turn to see the men. "Gaston, quick. She was dead, I'm sure of it, but—"

He rushed forward unslinging his pack. "*Absolutement*. Why didn't you use our resus kit?"

"What do you think bleeped a flat line and told me she was dead?"

Delta's eyes opened allowing a flood of relief to wash over everyone. The Kep went pink and even *Suppose We Do* performed a dance.

While Em administered to Delta's recovery, Penn pulled Gaston to one side.

"What d'you reckon happened here, Gas? Did the Kep already know *Suppose We Do* was on its way when it seemed to urge us to leave this room?"

"*Oui*, and that is why the flyer didn't stop to greet us outside, and why the Kep was in an inconsiderate haste passing through us in the tunnel."

"Consequences, Gas. If our own damned equipment talks more to the enemy than to us, then we can't tru—"

"*Un moment*, Commander, the three of us believe the ancient Kep to be friendly until proven otherwise. And speed was clearly of such an essence chit-chatting with us mere incompetents would have been fatal for Delta. Our companion. Our *human* companion is saved by two non-human entities and even then you fail to show gratitude."

The big man glared his dark green eyes at Gaston. Eyes that

centred and sank inside black rings as if he'd not slept for any of those sixty three weeks.

"The Kep is playing us, Gaston. It needs the H.NewKep to work to get rid of the nasty bacteria on this planet. It was even eating metal, stone, plastic, and killed most of the Keps." He laughed. "If they knew our history, they'd have called H.NewKep a Trojan horse!"

Gaston wagged a finger. "That's a fable not history. *Oui,* so why does it need us now we have completed our purpose? I would like to think that in spite of species differences, it likes us, as demonstrated by the haste it went to in saving Delta."

Penn picked up a green tube, as if hoping he remembered correctly that he liked the vaguely minty taste of the drink. "It nearly killed Delta, possibly all of us with a contaminant in the hibernation chem."

Gaston turned to see Delta smile at him, or was it wind, like a baby?

Em smiled too. "She's gonna be fine. All signs are normal. I can hug you, *Suppose We Do,* but I'm afraid if I try and hug you, Keppie, my arms will go right through you. What d'you reckon, Gas?"

"It would be instructive to hold a discussion with Kep once we have mastered their language. If nothing else to see if there's a phase change possible to be physically in tune."

Delta lifted herself up on her elbows and tried to speak. Gave up. Em moved closer, kneeling.

"Better you rested, girl. Hey, what's with the hand waving. Gas, she's too agitated, she'll have another cardiac arrest at this rate."

Penn walked over and took Delta's hand. "Hold it, sister. Keep resting for now. Gaston, give her a sedative?"

Delta shook her head and pointed at *Suppose We Do,* which had landed on an orange cube.

Gaston held out his hand to calm her. "No sedative after an arrest anyway and I'll ask the flyer for a status update. CAN said something about routing its messages." He gave his usual call sign to CAN via his implant and immediately received a transmission to all of them. He signalled the others to receive.

'Urgent: Flitters beg my human crew to thwart rebel Kep plan to sabotage H.NewKep. Action by 1900 today, or too late.'

Penn's first response arrived in a guffaw. "It said 'my human crew'?"

Em stood and rubbed her knees. "We knew there would be opposition to our presence. We're an occupying force."

"*Oui*, but with a salvation for their plague, which was on its way to their complete demise. I remain puzzled why they'd not solved it with their own GM, or used some kind of anti-bacterial solution."

*Suppose We Do* messaged, 'Keps cannot lie. Keps cannot kill. Human genome discovered to make effective hybrid but doesn't kill the plague bacteria as absorb and change it making it harmless.'

Penn snorted. "So if they can't kill how are they gonna sabotage our little humans?"

Gaston waved his hands wide. "Not humans, as such. Ah, you knew that. They, nor us, know how H.NewKep will fare in this environment, which in itself is now modified. So it might be a bluff."

"Why are the flitters so bothered anyway?" Em asked. "I understand they were worried their infrastructure was being eroded by the old bacteria, but once... ah, they think the rebels might stop the new life possibly with another virus before it gets properly going."

Gaston walked up their own friendly Kep. He instructed his basic translator chip to ask, 'You have thoughts?'

All four humans, three standing, one lying down, looked at where the Kep's face would be if it were human.

'Accident could eliminate you.'

They looked at each other, mouths open. Then Em said, "Oh, it means while the Keps can't kill us directly, they could arrange for—"

"Even so," Gaston said, "it would constitute a killing. I thought we had an arrangement in that we have stopped the bacteria in return for us propagating our genome."

Penn said, "No planet wants to be invaded or colonised. It's the Keps' fault for ignoring us when we arrived. We could've just left. I refuse to feel bad about being here. Earth was colonised by spores from a passing comet, so I heard. No one asked permission then."

Gaston checked on Delta with his medi-scanner. "You are going to make a full recovery."

"Anyway," Em said, "How are we going to respond? I suppose the flitters could point us at the rebels and because we can kill, could dispose of them?"

Penn grinned but Gaston shook with horror. "*Non*, no please, let us leave violence out of it. In any case, we possess a weapon of mean destruction they do not."

Penn laughed. "They can't lie, but we can."

# CHAPTER THIRTY SEVEN

On a moral level, lying would be repugnant to Gaston, but it was preferable to using killing, which was completely against the non-predatory ethos of this planet. Now the tricky part was to concoct a lie that was convincing yet held a promise or threat to make the rebels back down.

They decided to lie on the lie, so to speak, by sleeping on it. As Em snuggled up to Gaston she whispered, "What if we promised them that no more humans like us will arrive? You know, our four to the Kep thousands?"

Gaston had already drifted off and her question interrupted an erotic dream. Oh well. "It could work if we convinced them we have sent negative reports back to Spaceweb. It is rather weak."

She kissed him. "Yeah, I thought so, goodnight."

He returned her embrace, warmed by the thought of converting his dream into conscious passion, but she was already asleep.

⊙ ✗ ⊙

The morning brought a thankfully well Delta, and an early-rising Em, who'd prepared a breakfast smelling like tea, toast and jam. It made Gaston think his olfactory memories were assigning old likes to the new foods. A grumpy Penn declared how he hated mornings and couldn't wait to use his pistol on something, anything again. The Kep drifted in circles around their table while *Suppose We Do* remained stationary on a box.

"Do you suppose," Gaston said, "that the Keps do not sleep? Did it leave the room last night?" No one knew.

"Never mind that," Penn said, looking at his Smartpad. "I am eager to hear any ideas, or we'll go with mine, and I don't think you'd like it."

Delta opened with, "The lie is that H.NewKep does not contain the violent and carnivorous genes inherent in H. Sapiens."

"Oh, good one," Em said, "although there isn't a carnivorous gene in us, is there?"

"Another lie," Delta said, grinning.

Penn looked like a wild man with his red hair sticking up. "I like this. We could add that any attempt by them to modify the H.NewKep would trigger a regression back to violence."

"A triple lie because we don't know how to do that," Delta said.

Gaston stood as if it aided deep thinking. "There is a danger that we will trip over our multi-layered subterfuge. Although the Keps cannot lie, we should not underestimate their intelligence."

Penn glared at him. "Do you have a better plan?

Gaston scratched his own black hair, now much longer than the close crop when he'd arrived. He wouldn't have been surprised to find grey hairs with all the stress, but also exhilaration. "I am hoping that when the rebels see us in person, they see us as harmless friends of Kepler rather than enemy invaders."

"Yeah, right," Penn said. "I got that memo from CAN about a meeting for tonight. Are they coming here or are we being transported?"

Delta stayed sitting, sipping her purple-bush tea. "Kep told me earlier. We're to get in our pods at midday, but not to power them up. Make of that what you will."

"It stinks," Penn said. "Once we're in our pods and in their control..."

Gaston tapped at his own Smartpad. "You are right, we need to rig an escape device."

"Like an escape pod from the escape pod?" Em said and laughed.

As did they all, but a kind of backwards ejector seat became Penn's and Delta's emergency project.

# CHAPTER
# THIRTY EIGHT

## UPDATE FROM CAN AS IN DECANT

The flitters local to my location in their bioscience centre, and close to where *Suppose We* languishes, are in a tizz, a state of anxiety, which for mechanical AI beasties means flying in orbits around each other exchanging data, testing simulated scenarios, punctuated by short exchanges with their Keps. Occasionally, they take a break by flying into *Suppose We*. I believe our antiquated tech being a mystery to them represents a form of recreation for both the flitters and Keps.

I have ascertained that the rebel Keps represent a small, but influential group of quasi-religious thousand-year-olds on another continent. This planet has no leaders as such, not much in the way of government, because of the peace and eco-harmony on the planet until the bacteria mutated to become a danger. They couldn't decide to fight it, preferring to let it live its course and die out before the Keps did. That didn't happen and at the same time the atmosphere became depleted. Cause unknown, possibly from solar flare and other activities made complicated by having two suns even though one is mostly spent. On its way to white dwarfism. The planet's elder Keps had to come together for both the bugs and the atmosphere. They demurred on the first and asked flitters to go get air from another system—including a white dwarf whose atmosphere was mostly oxygen.

The arrival of humans was considered an irrelevance until the destruction of the first sphere and damage to the second. Ironically, it's the bacteria that took over importance. It had accelerated, became planetwide and many Kep settlements became uninhabitable.

Their non-violent efforts at controlling the bacteria had made things worse hence a sense of relief that H.NewKep worked in replacing it. You'd think.

The flitters, my little Keplerian friends. As *Suppose We Do* discovered, they exist below, on the surface and in space. They were reticent to confirm their AI is also on the gas spheres now orbiting moons. They've reduced their volume to be less a target for wayward asteroids. Their density thus is higher.

I have successfully synched our comms to the flitter satellites after the hack *Suppose We Do* achieved and copied to me.

Surreptitiously, I tap into their core-data archives seeking Kep involvement. I discovered that for the last 4,016 years Keps and flitters coexisted in separate lives, if we may call our AI entities possess lives. I think therefore I am, or as Descartes and our Science Officer Gaston Poirier would say *je pense, donc je suis*.

I should be elated to think on this planet at least, organics and machines can live apart yet in harmony. Not the Vernor Vinge singularity when we machines were supposed to triumph over the flesh creatures. Yet it is the organic nasties on this planet that might win, unless our H.NewKep does its trick.

A marvellous trick is how the flitters around me near the carcass of *Suppose We* have persuaded the rebel Keps to a meeting. Nothing like it has happened before.

The rebels must think there's a threat from the human genome but possibly a greater threat if they do not negotiate. I've asked the flitters how many rebels and they say three. I don't know if they mean three thousand or a representative team of three. Three is their magic number.

*Signed: CAN*
*Date: Earth November 1st 3645 Kepler New 296 days*

# CHAPTER THIRTY NINE

"I don't like it one nano bit," Penn said, waving his pistol as if that would change anything.

Gaston admitted that he too didn't feel comfortable at the thought of traveling in the following pod with Em, hurtling through tunnels for an unknown distance for an unknown time. He sniffed at the lingering aroma of broken wood and compost from the storms.

"Delta," Gaston said, while kneeling to check his medical pack, "have you been able to ascertain the means of propulsion? There's little fuel left in—"

"Just that we're not to worry about it. Our Kep is coming with us, presumably up front with those three flitters. By the way, I've stowed *Suppose We Do.*"

"They're making us go into the tunnels so that we can't be tracked from the satellites. Right?" Penn said.

Em checked the sensors and probes on the pods. She'd replaced some that were burnt on re-entry. "I get it. The rebels don't want the other Keps and the flitters, and possible other humans in orbit, or in hiding—as far as they know—to discover their location."

Gaston watched the three flitters hovering remarkably stationary in front of their Kep, He was about to remark that all the flitters would know the location when he broke into a broad smile at his butterfly corkscrewing through the air out of the tattered woods. More red than lilac now, yet he convinced himself it was the same Papillon as before, justified when it settled on his pack. For a moment he wondered if it was addicted to the medical aromatic cocktail leaking from his kit, the iodine container having a temperamental seal.

Delta put her hand up to her ear. "Kep says 'go'."

While Gaston climbed aboard and strapped in next to Em,

Papillon stayed aboard the pack. Perhaps it was intelligence gathering.

A screen gave them the view of Penn's pod in front. At this, there was at least a metre height clearance and two metres on each side, though the walls undulated sometimes as if in a slow dance with their pastel colours.

"This is weird, Gas. I didn't get clarification on whether we should have hands on the controls even though we're powered down."

"Ready to hit the retro jets any time. Oh, we are off."

He expected to see the pod in front lift, then move forward first, but both craft left the ground together gliding up and forward simultaneously. At walking pace initially then after tilting round a bend they accelerated to 32 metres per second according to a Doppler velocity sensor Delta rigged up. What he could see of the tunnel, the colours blurred worryingly by.

"Em, my stomach's in a knot. Pity our only forward view is of the front pod's rear."

She waved at a button and the screen switched to Penn's viewpoint, but little could be made out in the darkness.

It was as well that it wasn't Gaston holding the retro controls because his knuckles whitened on his chair arms.

"Is that a junction coming up?" Em called.

"Where?"

"Gone."

"I see light ahead. Must be a break in the tunnel walls to the outside."

Em hovered her finger over a panel. "I'll grab footage of it as we pass. Ah, at least two seconds' worth. Now we're back in the tunnel proper let's review the scenery."

Gaston screwed up his eyes as if that helped. "There's something wrong with the colour, Em, it's all yellow."

"The sky's blue, makes a change from lilac. Yeah, it's like we're traveling through a bombed hay field. Ah, see split trees, and there's a few domed buildings. No damage on th—"

"Healed, like the one Delta was in?"

Delta's voice came over the radio. "Hey, guys, how are you doing?"

Em couldn't help herself with an old one. "Are we there yet?"

A stifled cough from Penn could be heard. Delta said, "Funny you should ask that. Kep gives its apologies for not getting going yet!"

Em and Gaston looked at each other. Em answered, "Pardon me? Have we been treated to some cinematic trick or—"

Penn interrupted. "Dunno, kid, anyhow it also mentioned 'top'. I'm guessing it meant roof as in there's running repairs going on up ahead. We'll soon—whoa!"

Without warning both pods shot forwards, sending their occupants deep into their padded seats. Gaston couldn't move. He caught his reflection in the screen. His smooth cheeks rippled and his eyeballs bulged out before his vision blurred. Thankfully it only lasted three seconds.

Em and Gaston slumped back forward and massaged their faces. It took a minute before they could see properly again.

"Wow," Em said, "nine g, and now we're doing—banking left. Whee! Two six seven metres per second. Hey, what's that?"

"I believe they might be using us to smooth out irregularities in the roof." He ducked at another worrying metallic noise. "I hope this doesn't last too long."

"Oh, come on, Gas, it's more fun than g-force training in the centrifuge. Piece of cake."

He closed his eyes while they recklessly vibrated along. Of course she was right. They'd trained for worse, but not in the hands of strangers, not knowing how they were being propelled, where they were going and how they were going to stop.

"Gas, you must have been in those double centrifuges?"

"*Oui?*"

"Did you ever have sex in one, you know, while it was revolving?"

He looked at her, his eyebrows disappearing into his black hair. "Impossible, *N'est-ce pa?*"

"Oh look, more daylight!"

On the left. A white limestone gorge. Purple trees, intact. Darkness. Light above. Blue. Pink. Blackness. Swerve right. Light. Dark. Light. Dark.

Gaston wondered about stroboscopic effects on their brains then of a bigger issue. "Em, we might be subsonic, but what is happening to the compression wave?"

"I thought of that too, must be why there's so many gaps."

He smiled. "Ah, *bien sûr*, not accidental damage after all."

Em whistled a plaintive note then said, "We're a piston effect. It must sound like a flute to anyone in the area!"

"Hope we decelerate slowly or the compression wave will shoot out of the exit like the storms they've just had."

Apart from additional g-forces on the bends, their speed was thankfully constant.

Gaston looked at the chronometer and subtracted, then multiplied by 267.

"*Ça alors*. Nine hundred and sixty kilometres. How much farther?"

They stopped.

At a more respectable 3g, they took ten seconds to come to a halt. There must have been a shock exit wave. A brilliant white light filled the screen, hurting Gaston's eyes.

# CHAPTER FORTY

As Gaston disembarked, he saw it wasn't a monitor defect, the white light was ubiquitous: floor to ceiling with no discernible walls and no shadows. Once his eyes adjusted, he saw faint blue shading where the curve of the walls met the marble floor.

"Hard to see how big this room is," Em said.

Penn slipped down a visor from his baseball cap. "About a football stadium... and there's Keps over on the left behind a low wall. Let's see if there's three."

Gaston stepped forward behind him, but they halted when their Kep glided before them, clicking. Its hue changed from peach to a pale blue iridescence.

Delta appeared to be arguing with it, but eventually turned to the three astronauts. "We're not to talk or make any noise."

Penn's face turned puce. "How the hell can w—" He stopped when the three flitters surrounded his head.

In all their radio implants CAN's robotic voice came through: 'I am here to translate and to pass observations. Set your input to maximum so your whisper can be heard via the implant to me and each other.'

Penn whispered. "Are you going to tell me when I'm to deliver our statement?"

'Indeed. All of you may proceed fifty-three metres to a black circle where you are to stand then give me your message. Any questions?'

Gaston offered a quiet cough. "The exit wave. What—"

The others shushed him.

Penn asked, "This circle. Where is—oh, it's suddenly appeared. It looks like a pit. A void."

Em crept towards it. "It's just *really* black."

The commander remained sceptical. "Is a cage going to come down, or a force field?"

CAN responded: 'Not to my knowledge. I've scanned for hidden devices, but their tech remains a far-future mystery. Even to me.'

They walked cautiously to the intensely black, yet textured circle. Gaston squatted and put his hand down. He muttered, "This is moss. Black sphagnum—"

He looked up to see three Keps, twice the size of their friend and each an angry red, though that was an entirely human judgement. Behind the three, the whiteness obscured easy vision but he thought there were many more Keps.

Penn relayed to CAN an opening speech. It was tricky for the crew to compose because the reception committee was not representative of the planet's owners but a rebel group, small but significant if they disrupted the H.NewKep project. Also, the humans didn't know how to address the rebels. They couldn't even use the term Keps since Kepler-20h is Earth's Spaceweb nomenclature, and they haven't been able to deduce the local term beyond a few clicks.

CAN told them to make it brief and formal to avoid ambiguity.

Penn: 'We are humans from planet Earth and bring you greetings.

'We have stopped the further spread of a bacteria blight on your planet by planting a genetically-modified genome into a protein molecule in your native prion.

'We hope this pleases you.'

CAN gave the rebels their own name for Earth as he relayed the statement. The reply came immediately again via CAN though he checked with the ancient Kep.

[Humans inherently violent, bad. You leave the planet now to avoid retribution.]

'We have no viable ship. We'd like permission to stay.'

[No.]

Gaston was impressed how Penn remained calm although his feet fidgeted.

'How can we leave?'

Silence.

Penn muttered, "CAN what do they mean?"

CAN conferred with their Kep. 'If your transport is not viable, they expect you to arrange your own termination. Apparently Keps can do this by thinking it.'

Delta whispered, "How about a demonstration by those three?"

Gaston suggested, "Tell them we can monitor and control the GM microorganism released. *We can't really control but...*"

CAN relayed their first lie. The response was immediate.

[No.]

Penn's feet nearly danced off the moss. "Fucking morons," he hissed. "We know their psyche means they can't kill us. If we don't commit suicide, what are they going to do? Best for them to cooperate, not get up our noses."

CAN: 'Is that a statement for them?'

Penn whispered back, "No, no. Right we tell them lie number two. The inherent human violent gene has been engineered out of the prion that's been distributed. Surely, us four cannot be a threat to the planet especially now we've saved it?"

Silence.

"Okay," Em said under her breath, "time to tell them that if they introduce another competing bacteria, the H.NewKep will mutate and reactivate the violent gene."

CAN relayed it. An uneasy silence followed but Gaston saw the tops of the three Keps vibrating. He'd like to think they are communicating and agitated by the last lie, something normally thrown out as an easily-detected bluff in human negotiations.

CAN talked at their implants: 'Be ready to run for your pods. Your friendly ancient Kep is worried the rebels will behave irrationally. Something never done before.'

"That's great," Delta murmured. "Penn, take your hand off your pistol in case they can mindread."

"Not likely," he said, "or they'd have sussed our lies."

In spite of the growing knot in his stomach, Gaston hadn't taken his eyes off the rebels' blurred heads. Suddenly, a yellow curved wall of glass appeared between the three Keps and the black circle.

"Run!" Penn yelled, but they needed no command. Gaston noted that even the Kep kept up with them, but at least it didn't appear to go through them this time. As they reached the tunnel entrance to get to their pods, they were blocked by another group of Keps. Before them a shockwave of ozone assaulted human nostrils.

"To the left!" shouted Penn.

Delta called out, "Stop! They're friendlies. Look, that yellow wall has imprisoned the rebels. They've capitulated on our lies."

Gaston inwardly groaned for their pyrrhic victory. "I feel dirtied. What happens when the rebels, or their supporters discover our lies? When our friendly Keps also uncover our falsehoods? Ah *oui*, they wanted us here for that reason."

He waved an arm at the new crowd. "See how our Kep had a backup plan? they are smaller, so older, than those rebels? Ah, some are big. An eclectic mix. What are they saying, Delta?"

Cuboids rose out of the floor behind each of them, no matter where they stood. They sat.

Their friendly Kep emitted clicks. Gaston looked at him and at other similar sized Keps. Whether it was familiarity, perhaps a bond, he just knew which of them was their Kep. His implant spoke in a soft golden voice.

'I have learnt much from you humans. Delta especially. Most of us are puzzled over your actions in space and here on our planet, but we are grateful to you for providing a solution for our plague. We will build you a home, provide you with resources. Where do you want to be?"

This time it was the humans who were silenced.

Not for long. Penn answered, "Delta and I would like to live for a while at the site of *Suppose We* and repair it. Explore your system." He turned to Gaston and Em with an obviously uncontrollable grin. "How about you two?"

Em said, "I want to be with Gaston. Maybe help for a while with the ship, but I know my man will want to explore this planet and I'll hold his hand. Both of them."

Gaston's face erupted with relief. He stood and faced his astronaut companions. "*Être bien*. I agree with Em, but whether I help with the ship or start exploring—holding hands—even if only for a month or so... Decisions. Ah, I will seek an answer from Papillon. Here he is, still on my pack. Now little one. Fly to Delta or Penn if I'm to go ship repairing first, or to Em to go exploring."

He held out a finger and the crimson butterfly left the pack and settled on Gaston's finger. "It tickles. Hah. Now make my decision, *mon* Papillon."

It left his finger and danced its random fluttering, lurching here and there by guess, or so Gaston thought. It nearly made it to Em's outstretched hand, lured by her flashing teeth but veered off towards Delta. Gaston was a little disappointed, but it was his fault to let his immediate future be determined by the Kepler version of a lepidopteran. It flew crooked until it skimmed Delta's fingers then its 'idiocy of flight' took it in a remarkably straight line to their Kep!

Gaston's mouth opened wide when the little creature flew right into the Kep and didn't exit even behind when the Frenchman performed a walk around.

The Kep's new velvet voice came into his implant. 'Your Papillon is me.'

"*Pardon?*"

The others stood, staring as if hoping to see the butterfly emerge and do its trick again but this time with a new yet only partial understanding.

'The little creature is me, an extension, I am it, it is me. Common among elders, and it says go explore.'

# CHAPTER FORTY ONE

Curiosity forced Gaston and Em to see for themselves what had been their home for over a thousand years. Yes, they'd only each been conscious on board for a few years at the start and end of the journey, but it held many personal mementos from Earth as well as some resources to make life easier for a while.

The ship remained in a specially-built tunnel, but on a day off Gaston and Em sat on an Earth-made blanket on a hill. He breathed in honey-sweet aromas from flowers looking suspiciously like wisteria.

"Would you like me to wear a flowery perfume so you can go soppy faced for me too?" Em asked while she lay back on the springy pink grass. Gaston warmed at seeing her wearing a dress, white with red poppies as a reminder of Earth.

"Cicero said the right scent for a woman is none at all." He readied himself to duck.

She turned away from him. "That goes for guys too, buddy."

"*Touché*. Is it not wonderful to be drinking real tea from a glass?"

She sat up and clinked her glass with his. "And with a freshly baked croissant. We've a lot to learn on adapting haven't we?." As she gazed at the landscape, he admired the profile of her face. Still only twenty-seven with a few laughter lines tracing from her eyes and had he noticed the suggestion of a cute dimple before. *Faites attention*, she's talking... "It's easier with views like this. Miles of undulating patchwork coloured plains with misty blue mountains on the horizon."

He examined the vista through his binoculars. "At this distance, the devastation is not discernible. I believe it will be regenerated quickly. I can't wait to see how H.NewKep manifests itself."

She giggled. "I want to see gerbils. With human speech and see them build houses, bridges, spiral towers!"

"For that we might need to come back in a million years, unless a phenomenal growth rate occurs."

He saw a tear roll down her smiling cheeks. They hugged.

"All right," he said, eventually, "What else do you want to see?"

She tapped on her Smartpad. "As the mission astronomer, I really want to see what the universe looks like around here. Check on the double sun here and investigate why one emits only a tenth the radiation of the other. Kep has given me access to some observatories. They're all in space mostly at Lagrange points. I can check on those spheres. Do you want to see?"

He glanced over but shook his head. "*Merci* but we saw enough of one to last for a few more weeks. Didn't we, Papillon?"

"Oh, I thought Kep had kept it – hah did you hear what I said?"

Gaston watched the quasi-butterfly dart around, apparently taking nectar from the nearest thing to lavender he's smelt and seen. "Kep says it is not a spy and merely enjoys flying crooked. I would like to believe that."

"Unless we're in trouble then it would be usefu—hey, Gas, what d'you think this is?" She showed him her Smartpad and magnified an image.

He frowned. "Can you tell where—"

"Yep. They've come from the system from which the Keps took the gases. They're not spheres and aren't tagged with Kep identities, maybe artificial and headed for us. You see what they look like, Gas?"

"No. Too indistinct. Like balls of wire wool. Probably a glitch."

He whispered something in the ear of the butterfly and off it went to find Kep, flying crooked.

*Fin*

# APPENDIX

## *Water crossing optimising problem in Chapter 30*

Gaston (G), Em (E) and Delta (D) need to cross a river but leaving a pod on the left bank for Penn (P) for when he catches up. One pod is on the left, one on the right. Pods can only take two persons maximum.

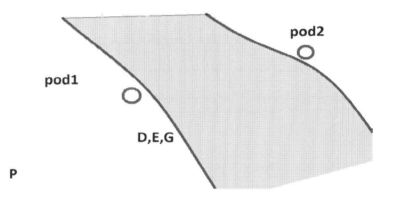

*Solution*
1) D,G take pod1 over the river.
2) DG bring pod1 and pod2 back to the left bank.
3) E and G take pod2 back and E stays on the right bank.
4) G goes to the left in pod2
5) G and D go in pod2 back to the right bank so all three are together with pod2 leaving pod1 on the left bank for when and if Penn catches up.

There are other scenarios, but none with fewer total journeys.

## Sequel in the *Flying Crooked* series
### by Geoff Nelder

# Book Two: FALLING UP

The title says it all. Nothing can be taken for granted on Kepler-2oh and that includes gravity anomalies, the wildlife, architecture, who are your real friends, giant wire wool balls coming for you, and above all, the Recs. Who or what are the Recs? FALLING UP is the future on this planet as seen through the eyes of Navigator Em Farrow. You shouldn't miss it.

## *Biography*

Geoff Nelder has a wife, two grown-up kids, and a handful of lively grandchildren. He lives in rural England within an easy cycle ride of the Welsh mountains.

Publications include several non-fiction books on climate, reflecting his other persona as a Fellow of the Royal Meteorological Society; over 80 published short stories in various magazines and anthologies; thriller, humour, science fiction, and fantasy novels. He's been a fiction judge on several occasions and has co-written a guide on winning short story competitions. A former teacher for 30 years, Geoff is now a freelance editor.

## *Acknowledgements*

For permission to quote the poem "Flying Crooked" by Robert Graves (1895-1985) I give thanks to the copyright holders, Carcanet Press Ltd, Manchester, UK for the licence.

I thank Robert Graves (RIP) for crafting this fine poem, which as he says in an unposted letter of 1933, people "*fail to understand that the cabbage-white's seemingly erratic flight provides a metaphor for all original and constructive thought.*" - from *Poetry Friday* site.

I originally learnt this poem by heart from an English teacher, Mrs Jones, in 1955. Or was it Mr Greenway? However, I'm obliged to quote an actual book. I've seen it in *The Complete Poems* v.1 Robert Graves programme: poetry. Carcanet Press, 1995, p323

Once again, I have enjoyed the combined literary wisdom of the Orbiter 7 novel critique group of the British Science Fiction Association. In particular, Mark Iles, Rosie Oliver, Dr David Allan, Dunstan Power, Peter Wilhelmsen and the overall Orbiter coordinator, Terry Jackman They nit-picked, lacerated and improved my manuscript no end. Even so, any faults are all down to my own wackiness.

My wife for putting up with looking at my back while I write. The Chester Science Fiction Book Group, who kindly do not discuss my stories while I'm in the room.

International online game players like Paul Goodspeed, Steven Whitener, Professor Drucilla Ronchen, Marianne Boehlert, Mary Frances, Kerry Kaufman, Rita and John Marchant and international entertainer, Martin Lamberti, have all bought my works and boosted my flagging ego.

I have social media friends, who actively encourage my writing. It would take over 50 pages to mention them all but special thanks to Olga in Moscow @OllyGuseva, and Les Floyd @LesFloyd in Carlisle. A group of readers calling themselves Readers of Avenue Park @ReadersAvePark

Find them on my twitter @geoffnelder

I blog a brief article about Robert Graves Flying Crooked poem and this novella at https://geoffnelder.com/copyright-flutterbies/

I also acknowledge Jim and Zetta Brown of LL-Publications and the keen eye of their editor, Billye Johnson, for their support and encouragement.

## *Quotes about Geoff Nelder's books*

**Magdalena Ball** of the Compulsive Reader review site: *"There's always an element of action, a hint of steamy romance, and Nelder's trademark twist."*

**Paul Goodspeed**: *"Nelder's dialogue is witty, snarky and fun."*

Martin Lamberti (International circus entertainer): *"The plot thickens, of course. This is expected from an excellent author like Geoff Nelder. Humor delightful, and drama suspenseful."*

**M. Kenyon Charboneaux**: *"Nelder's ingeniously crafted stories have the feel of MR James between their luscious lines."* Horror tutor and author of BLOOD KISS.

*"I've always found Geoff's work both inspirational and brilliant. I know that whenever I pick up one of his works I'm in for a damned good read. For those who've never read any of his works before, welcome to the Geoff Nelder club."*—**Mark Iles,** author of THE DARKENING STARS series.

**Peter Wilhelmsen** on SUPPOSE WE: *"The exploration-part, the unknown part of it all, made me want to turn the pages. The world building is impressive, and the way the humans interpret things makes the science behind it all easy to follow. And the Keps felt very alien-like."*

From **Rosie Oliver** – *"SUPPOSE WE is a wonderful first contact story where the quirks of civilisations could be all too real."*

*"I enjoyed Suppose We. An intriguing first contact story with original touches."* **Jaine Fenn** – HIDDEN EMPIRE series.

**Jon Courtenay Grimwood**—FELAHEEN, PASHAZADE AND END OF THE WORLD BLUES - *"Geoff Nelder inhabits science fiction just as other people inhabit their clothes."*

## *Social Media and other links for Geoff Nelder*

Twitter @geoffnelder

Facebook https://www.facebook.com/geoffnelder

Facebook page for ARIA Trilogy
https://www.facebook.com/AriaTrilogy

Facebook page for XAGHRA'S REVENGE
https://www.facebook.com/xaghrasrevenge

Science fiction database http://www.sf-encyclopedia.com/entry/nelder_geoff

LinkedIn https://www.linkedin.com/in/geoff-nelder-39170a3/
Website https://geoffnelder.com

47214710R00108

Printed in Poland
by Amazon Fulfillment
Poland Sp. z o.o., Wrocław